Sacred Hills Massacre

All Conroy and Kincade wanted was enough gold to build the ranch they dreamed of. Old Angus Newell took them into the Black Hills hoping they'd come back with gold enough for that ranch, somewhere he could spend the rest of his days sitting in front of the fire.

Margaret Baldwin went into the Black Hills to find who killed her uncle. Bart Starkey guided her, wanting to get his hands on all the gold. The Lakota Sioux warrior, Blackhand, just wanted to kill the white men whose presence violated the sacred land.

These people rode into what Indians called *Paha Sapa* or Sacred Hills and the white men knew as the Black Hills, for different reasons. A few got what they wanted, others got what they deserved.

Sacred Hills Massacre

J.D. Ryder

A Black Horse Western

ROBERT HALE · LONDON

© William Sheehy 2008
First published in Great Britain 2008

ISBN 978-0-7090-8635-2

Robert Hale Limited
Clerkenwell House
Clerkenwell Green
London EC1R 0HT

www.halebooks.com

Typeset by
Derek Doyle & Associates, Shaw Heath
Printed and bound in Great Britain by
CPI Antony Rowe, Chippenham, Wiltshire

CHAPTER ONE

The three white men tensed as they watched the string of Lakota Sioux warriors ride by. Outnumbered, the men crouched behind the half-decayed spruce log. Armed with Henry carbines, they would give a good account of themselves if discovered, but it would be a losing battle. Only after the last rider disappeared down the hillside did the men let themselves exhale long-held breath.

'You see the leader?' Angus Newell asked, still keeping his eyes on where the Indians had gone. 'That was Blackhand, I swear. He's a bad one.'

The others waited silently until Newell nodded and, placing a hand on the tree trunk, pushed himself up. 'I reckon they're gone, so it's probably a good time for us to light a shuck our own selves. They're riding down where we just come up and it wouldn't surprise me none if one of them sharp-eyed cusses didn't spot some mark we left along the trail.'

Followed closely, he led the way back into the forest to the little gully where they'd left their horses.

'How'd you come to hear them coming?' the youngest of the three asked as they mounted up. Sitting his saddle with his Henry lying across his thighs Newell kept watch on the tree-covered slope they'd just come down.

'Didn't. It was the birds going quiet that warned me. For some time now there's been a couple crows cawing and carrying on. We didn't bother them none, probably got used to us. But those bucks on their horses, well, the birds noticed them and shut up.'

The Sioux braves weren't the first Indians Con Conroy had ever seen but always before it had been the one of two blanket-wrapped old men hanging around the outside of a white man's building. He didn't want to have to face these red men.

'You say their leader was Blackhand?' Kincade asked, his voice raspy but still sounding soft. 'I seem to have heard that name before.'

'Yeah, that was him. I saw him once when old Spotted Tail was brought in to talk with the Yankee soldiers. A young brave just learning all he could about the hated white eyes. Wagh! Them boys you just saw'd lift your hair in a heartbeat, if'n they knew we was hiding up here.'

'What are we going to do? You figure there's more of them around here somewhere?' Con asked, scanning behind them.

'Hard to say 'xactly where, but you can bet the rest of the band is somewheres not far away, that's for sure. This time of season, they're likely heading south into buffalo country for the annual hunt.' Reining his scruffy-looking mustang around, he sat back in his scarred saddle.

'This time of year,' Newell went on after a bit, 'I reckon they're headed south, going down to some place like Buffalo Gap or the Devil's Tower or maybe Bear Butte. It's the Lakota Sioux what travel through these Black Hills. Oh, others do too. Some Arapaho and Cheyenne, but it's the Lakota you got to watch out for. Call themselves The People and have this belief that no humans should be living in the *Paha Sapa*, what we call the Black Hills. All this part of the country is sacred to most tribes. They come up in these hills to purify themselves and look for their personal vision. For as long as anyone knows, these hills was only for the birds and the animals, not for humans.'

That was the way it was, Con had learned, ask the old-timer a question and then, for the next stretch of time, listen to the answer.

'But that only means we'll have to be a mite

more careful. Them Lakota warriors can be a mean bunch. Most times, up here in the hills, they won't bother other redskins. It's like an unwritten law, there ain't no fighting. It is all sacred land. That don't hold for any whites they catch, however. White eyes don't count.'

Motioning with one hand, Newell jabbed a heel against the mustang's side. 'Be best, I figure, if from now on we stayed away from even the faintest of game trails. C'mon. I reckon we can get over this ridge and down the other side before we start looking for a place to spend the night.'

Nothing else was said as the three men threaded their way through the trees. Con, bringing up the rear, continued to twist in the saddle, looking over his shoulder. He was a lot younger that the others. He was a tall man, standing an inch over six foot, with a raw-boned face and flashing blue eyes and a full head of black hair. After being on the trail for nearly two weeks, the hair was only slightly cleaner-looking than what he'd seen on the heads of the Indians who had just gone by. Unlike those wild men, his hair was held out of his eyes under a weather-grayed floppy Stetson.

Until a few weeks ago, he'd been a cowman. Raised on his pa's ranch, Con was one of five boys. When his father died, the eldest son took over the ranch and rather than spend the rest of his life working as a cowhand for his brother he left to

8

make his own way in the world. When he rode away from the Double C, old Kincade had called for his pay and gone along.

As far back as he could remember, Kincade had been there, showing the youngest of the Conroy boys how things were done. Looking at his back, now a few yards ahead, Con smiled. His pa had been too busy to teach any of the boys how to ride or work a ranch. For young Con it had been Kincade who was his teacher, showing, mostly by example, how to toss his loop, ride a wild bronco and even shoot a revolver. Being five years younger than the next brother, he hadn't paid much attention to how they learned cowboying, all his attention was on pleasing Kincade.

He'd always thought of the older man as being, well, old. That was before they met up with Angus Newell. It was hard to tell the old-timer's age, but looking at his sun- and wind-burned wrinkled face and near hairless scalp, it was clear that he was really old.

To hear him tell it, he'd been all over this country, clear out to the ocean and up into Oregon Territory. It was while listening to him tell his tall tales that Con had heard the Black Hills and gold mentioned. That was when the young man decided to throw in with the old man in the search of that gold . . . not to get rich, but enough to buy his own cattle ranch.

Blackhand wasn't happy with the men he'd been given to make this hunt. They were all untried boys and this was their first real hunt without some of the older, more experienced braves along. It wasn't his first hunt and he was sure he'd been better prepared when he had followed his uncle Black Elk. But the band needed meat. They had been traveling since the snow began to melt and were still a week's ride from the edge of the buffalo grasslands. There should be deer coming to water at the creek below this late in the afternoon.

'*Hola*, Blackhand.' It was Honovi, the Sioux word for Strong Deer and a name that made Blackhand laugh inside. Honovi had been the first one to call for stopping for water at the tiny creek they had crossed a brief time ago. Always complaining about something.

'What?' Blackhand didn't stop or even look around.

'It is time we stopped to rest the horses. Eating dried meat and berries is bad enough, but to do it while rushing ahead is worse.'

'Honovi, whether we stop or keep going, that's all we have to eat. The horses don't need to rest, they've only been walking, not running. We will stop when we get closer to the stream down below.'

'What stream? How do you know of this stream

and what difference does it make, your stream down below or that one back there?'

For a long moment Blackhand didn't answer. Then when he thought enough time had passed he spoke, again not looking back. 'The stream at the bottom of this ridge is wide and slow-moving. I know it from when I hunted it before with Black Elk. The little creek we passed didn't have good deer grazing. Now ride quietly.'

Someone had not done a good job in teaching these youngsters, Blackhand thought. They had no respect for the sacred lands they were riding through and little knowledge about hunting.

The trail they had been following wasn't more than a two-hand-span wide, a game trail that over the seasons had been used by The People and others. He hoped his memory was good and this was the way to the stream he and his uncle had hunted the previous fall.

After the long winter the deer wouldn't be as fat as they had been that time but the venison would be welcome. Bringing in three or four would feed the band for a few more days and in that time they would be close to the grasslands.

Visions of the coming buffalo hunt vanished when he spotted the scuff mark in the dirt ahead. Pulling on the reins he stopped his horse and was off in the same movement. Faintly, he could see the print, made by a leather boot heel, not the soft indentation of a moccasin.

'What are you stopping for?' Honovi called. 'Change your mind about resting the horses?' Blackhand heard his soft chuckle.

'Stay there,' he ordered, tying the reins to a branch of a tree. Careful not to step in the prints, he walked ahead, head down, eyes sweeping the narrow trail. There, a second scratch in the earth made by an iron horseshoe. A few other times he'd seen marks like that, marks left by a shod horse; only white men put iron on the hoofs of their horses. From the sharp edges of one print he saw that it had been made very recently. Not too long ago a white man had ridden up this trail.

Standing straight, he looked down toward the bottom of the slope. From where he stood he caught his first glimpse of the meadow. This was the right place. Thinking about the prints, he made his decision.

'Mahpee.' He called another of the hunters. Another strong name for an inexperienced young man, but the only one of this group who Blackhand thought, showed any leadership traits.

'Yes, what have you seen?'

'I believe it is the print of a white man. Below is the meadow I was heading for,' he said, pointing through the last of the trees. 'Will you lead these fine hunters down there? Stop before leaving the trees and tie off the horses. Let Honovi be your horse holder. Spread everyone out in the grass and wait for the deer to come to water. That will be as the sun is going behind the trees.'

'What will you do?'

'I will go back to see if I can find the white man. The band needs meat so be good hunters. Can you do this thing?'

Mahpee, or Sky, stood looking down at the bottom of the slope, studying his response. 'It will be good if we can kill many deer. If not, then it will be bad for the leader to return empty handed.'

Blackhand nodded. He understood what Mahpee was saying. He'd go but he wouldn't take the blame if things went bad. So be it. To capture or kill the white man trespassing in these hills that had been blessed for as long as man walked was, he thought, more important.

'I will take Ahahy with me,' Blackhand said and turned back to his horse.

Without explaining, Blackhand motioned for Ahahy to follow and led his horse back up the game trail. Somewhere ahead of them was a man he was going to kill.

CHAPTER TWO

After leaving the family ranch in Texas, Con and Kincade had hired on with a cattle drive to a ranch north of Kansas into the Indian Territory. He had started as a hand at fifteen; now, ten years later he thought it was time to be finding his own spread and maybe start his own family. When he'd talked to Kincade about it, the older man agreed but pointed out that it took money to start a ranch, more than they could earn working another man's cattle. When they heard about a gold strike further north on the South Platte River, the two men thought they'd give it a look.

The Cherry Creek diggings had proved valuable for a few men. William Russell hadn't gotten rich over in the California diggings, but he found enough placer gold on Cherry Creek to make him happy. When Con and Kincade got there they found two kinds of men trying to make a strike,

14

those like Russell who dug for gold and the other kind, those who took advantage of them. Hold-ups and killings were reported to be happening every day. Russell's new camp, given the elegant name of Denver City, had been built near the claim the man had marked out. Like most gold rush communities, it was mostly tents and log lean-tos. From what Kincade said, it wouldn't likely last long, neither the gold nor the town.

A few years back, when news of the gold discoveries over in California had reached the Double C, Kincade and a few others had drawn their time and joined a wagon train west. Two years later, just before winter hit the Texas plains, Kincade came back explaining how most of the rivers had claims running up and down both banks and hundreds of men working them. Few were finding real gold though. Not like the newspapers had said. Kincade came back with only the clothes on his back. He was given his job back and rode a borrowed saddle for the next year or so.

He had to laugh when Con suggested they ride up into the Black Hills to look for gold.

But the story handed out by the old man, Newell, had sounded pretty good. It was something, the way they met up with the old man. Leaving Denver City, he and Con had hired on to ride shotgun on the stage to Fort Laramie. With one riding facing back and the other sitting next to the man with the reins, they found themselves protecting the US Army payroll box which was lashed between them.

The money offered to make that run was more than they had made trailing cattle, but still not enough to think of going into ranching. But that was how they ended up in Fort Laramie, on the high seat of a rough riding, leather-slung stage-coach. Later, lining up at the long mahogany bar in the Sutler's Saloon, they were once again considering their options when they overheard an old man talking.

'Yeah, I could tell you stories about them hills. I been all over them. You doubt me, you young pup?' he asked when one of the soldiers standing next to him laughed. 'Wal, let me tell you, I wasn't much older than you when I went traipsing through with old Jedediah Smith. Then when the govermit sent out Captain Reynolds and that man what called hisself a doctor, Hayden was his name, to map out what they called the Black Hills. Wal, I went along as a guide, don't you know. Yes, sir, I do know about that part of the country.'

Con saw that the old-timer was just about falling down drunk. He felt a little sad, feeling that if he didn't find something soon, that could be his future. When the crowd of young men who had been goading the old man seemed bent on contin-uing their game, he stepped in.

'Now boys, I guess you've had your fun,' he said in a quiet voice. Standing as he was, not letting his smile reach his cold eyes and with one hand on the butt of his holstered Navy Colt, he didn't think they would argue. 'Why don't you just go about your business and let me take care of this old fella.'

The argument came from the old-timer. 'Say, there,' he swung around, almost falling over as he moved, 'what the hell d'ya think you're doing? Them boys ain't doing nobody no harm and they been mighty free with their bottle.'

Con heard Kincade chuckle but ignored it. 'Well,' he said, holding up his hand and smiling to show the old man he meant no harm. 'Maybe I did step in where it wasn't wanted. But I wanted to hear more about your travels up north. Come on, I'll buy you lunch and you can tell me all about those Black Hills you mentioned.'

Somewhere down the line, he couldn't remember where, he'd heard someone talking about the Black Hills. It seemed from what he could recall, someone was said to have found gold up there. At the time he thought it was just another of those lost gold mine tales that the West seemed to be full of. Getting some food and coffee into the old man probably wouldn't change much, but Con hated to see any man drunk as a fiddler's clerk so early in the day. Maybe, he thought, as the three men left the saloon, two walking straight and holding up the third, he should get a Bible and take up preaching.

'Now young man, don't think I ain't aware what those young pups was throwing off on me,' the old-timer said, leaning heavily on Con's arm as they pushed into a nearby restaurant. 'But they was some interested in what I've seen and where I'd been.'

'A good meal and one of us'll feel a lot better, old-timer,' was all Con could think of to say.

'Yeah, I guess to look at me you'd figure I was up the spout, too old to be any good for anything. But that's only today. Yesterday and tomarra I won't be drunk and then you'll see I can still cut the mustard.'

After ordering plates of the lunch special and coffee, the three men sat and looked at each other.

'Was you really interested in those Black Hills, or was you just funnin' me.'

'Tell the truth, I did hear something about them one time. Can't recall exactly what it was, though.'

The old man chuckled and took a sip of coffee. Con lifted his cup but put it back down, it was still to hot to drink.

'I'm Newell, Angus Newell.'

'Carl Conroy,' said Con, shaking the older man's hand, 'named after my pa. Mostly I just answer to Con. And the silent one here is my partner, Kincade.'

'Well, happy to make your acquaintance, I'm sure. And I bet what you heard about that part of the country was the gold that some dude said he found up there. That's what everybody's wanting to know about.'

Con tried his coffee again but didn't drink. How the old man could handle that hot liquid was beyond him. The heat didn't seem to bother Kincade, either.

'Is there gold up there?' Kincade asked, breaking his silence.

'Oh, I reckon there is. It's certain that if there is it'll likely stay there. One thing nobody seems to pay any mind to is that there's a heap of Indians in those mountains and they don't like white eyes hanging around. It's sacred ground to them.'

Con frowned. 'But you said you've been there, alongside a couple others. How'd you do that without causing trouble?'

'By being damn careful. Let me tell you, it weren't easy.'

Throughout the meal Newell talked about the Black Hills and the more he talked the more interested Con become.

After paying for the meal, the men stood on the plank walk outside the restaurant.

'You seem mighty interested in gold, young fella,' Newell said, chewing on a wooden toothpick he'd taken from a bowl on the table.

'I guess I am. A little gold would fit right nice in my pocket about now. Somehow I'd like to be able to stop working for the other man and get my own spread. There's a lot of land a mite south of here that'd be fine for raising cattle and a family, I reckon. But I haven't figured out how to make it all work.'

Newell, standing straight and sober, all of five feet tall in his run-over-at-the-heel boots, nodded. 'Yes, that's what we all want, isn't it? A nice piece of land, a snug cabin and a warm fireplace in the winter.'

That was how it all began, Con Conroy thought as he and Kincade followed Newell up and over the top of the ridge and, still weaving in and out of the thin forest, down the other side.

It hadn't been hard to talk Newell into going along as a guide. Once Con agreed to pay for the supplies the old man only asked for one thing.

'By gob, that sounds all right. I'll take you two back up into those hills and we can do our looking. You'll see why those pesky redskins think it's all so special but I ain't promising we'll come back rich men. Either of you know anything about prospecting for gold?'

Leaning against the top rail of the corral back of the town livery stable, they were careful not to let anyone overhear their plans. Gold, or the thought of gold, Kincade pointed out, made people act funny. Best, he advised, to keep their plans to themselves.

'Well, I don't,' said Con, then nodding his head toward Kincade. 'But he's been out to California and saw how things worked out there.'

'And come back with empty pockets, don't forget.' Kincade chuckled.

'All right,' Newell said, nodding his decision. 'I'll tell you my offer. We'll go up in there and, if we're a mite careful, we'll come back out. That's not to say we'll be carrying gold, but if we are it all gets split between the two of you.'

'That doesn't make sense.' Con shook his head.

'Yeah, it does. You say you want to set up ranching. Well, my share will go to helping you do just that and be the buy-in for me. A place to spend the rest of my days like you said, somewhere with a fire in winter and where I don't have to eat restaurant food or anything I have to fix for myself. Now, what do you say, we got a deal?'

After a moment's hesitation the three men shook on it.

Riding out of town Newell pointed them in a southerly direction. After a full day's ride he led them off the main wagon road and through the brush, the start of a wide circle. Following game trails, they were soon heading back in a north-west-

21

erly direction. After supper the second night, as they were leaning back and relaxed over a final cup of coffee, Newell started to talk about what was coming.

'Another day or so we'll be close by Bear Butte. That's a mountain of bare rock that towers up above the trees and can be seen for miles. A little west of that is Dark Canyon. That's what old Jedediah marked it, anyhow. I think he was making a joke cuz the canyon is really a broad flat valley with sandstone walls standing straight up on either side. That's about where we'll start climbing up into the forest. I figure we'll set up a camp in a little meadow I saw once, and start our search. We can ride in but whatever gold there'll be to find will be in the sand and gravel of some pretty wild creeks and that means a lot of traveling on foot. That's why I had you buy those moccasins from that old Indian woman there at the fort. Those high-heeled boots you're wearing won't be so good for climbing over rocks or wading in the water, now will they?'

Both Kincade and Con had been quietly following behind their guide, happily taking in the beauty of the mountain valley they were riding out of. That was when Newell pulled back on the reins.

'What. . . ?' Con started to say but stopped when Newell waved a hand at him.

'Quick.' He motioned to a little ravine on the

uphill side of the trail they'd been following. 'Up there and don't make any more noise than you have to. Hurry now,' he directed, herding the party up and into the brush.

Most of the forest floor they were now riding through was layered by a thick carpet of pine needles. After dropping over a rocky ridgetop, Newell pointed toward a little depression.

'Tie the horses off there and bring your rifles. Quiet, now,' he ordered, and led the way back up and down to where they could see through the trees the game trail they'd just left.

Silence filled the forest and Con was about to ask why, when the first Indian rode into view on the trail below them.

Somehow he hadn't doubted Newell's warning talk about there being Indians up in these mountains, but the bunch that went riding by made Con a firm believer. Thinking about the danger those warriors posed, he now paid close attention to the slope and forest behind them. Now riding in single file with Newell again in the lead, they proceeded silently for a while until, coming up to a small stream of sparkling water, Newell swung out of the saddle. Con noted that nobody had slid his rifle back into a saddle case.

'Maybe they won't see any sign of our passing,' Newell said, letting his horse drink. 'But we'll keep to these upper ranges for a while. As I recollect, on the other side of that next ridge there's a little pocket of a meadow. As good a place as any to spend the night and be far enough from the trail those Indians would be using.'

Having watered the horses and again making their way through the trees, it seemed to Con that having a goal somehow made the ride a little easier. Maybe, he thought, it was because the fear he'd felt had started to ease.

Angus Newell was a couple yards ahead of the two men, keeping his horse at a walk. Thinking back to the Indians, it was a complete shock when Con was knocked off his horse by a smashing blow. As the young man landed flat on his back Newell was shocked to see the feathered end of an arrow sticking out of his shoulder.

'Stay down, boy,' Newell called.

As the pain started shooting across his body, Con lay back, looking up through the treetops at the blue sky. Everything was silent. It was almost, he thought, as though he was all alone. But the arrow had had to come from somewhere. Thinking about there being Indians sneaking around made him want to hide, but it hurt to move. The best he could do was to slowly thumb the thong that held his revolver in the holster and bring the Navy Colt up. He flicked off the safety and waited, ready.

For a long time stillness filled the forest. When

the sound of first one then another rifle being fired shattered the quiet, it made Con's body stiffen. After the shots, silence fell again.

'I think they've gone, Con,' Kincade said quietly. 'How bad you hit, can you tell?'

'There's an arrow through my shoulder. Guess I've been afraid to move. Did your shots scare them away?'

'Bah, that's about all I could do, was shoot to scare. I couldn't see a blamed thing to shoot at.'

'Well,' Newell said as he came sliding down the slope, 'one of us shot true. But I think there was at least one, maybe two. I went across there where they had set their ambush and found blood, so I know one of the buggers was hit. There's no sign of them now. I reckon they pulled away, I know that's what I'd do. Ain't no place we can go they can't find us when they want. C'mon, let's take a look at that shoulder.'

Slowly sitting up, Newell saw that the arrow had torn through the muscle of the young man's upper arm. The thin beaten iron arrowhead and a couple inches of the shaft were completely on the back side.

'I reckon it missed the bone and just cut through the muscle,' Newell said. 'You was mighty lucky. I'll cut that point off and we can pull the arrow out. It's probably going to hurt a mite.'

Con didn't howl with pain but he certainly

25

wanted to. 'Damn it, man, if that's a mite I'd hate to have to deal with any more.'

'Ah, wal, I reckon. Now talking about pain,' he started in talking while using his belt knife to cut a piece of Con's shirt away. 'I recollect one time, it was while trapping with old Jim Bridger it was, when a redskin got an arrow into the thigh of another trapper that was along. Same as yourn, it was, missed the bone and went clear through.' Using the strip of cloth from Con's shirt he wrapped the shoulder as tightly as he could. 'That'll help slow down the bleeding. Yeah, course it hurt, just like my trapper friend was hurt. But what hurt him more was that the poor man had to walk back to where we was camped. All you gotta do is get back on that horse of you and follow us on over the ridge. You're mighty lucky.'

Con was too proud to complain after that and followed along quietly.

It was coming on to dark when Newell at last called a halt. Since being shot Con hadn't been paying too much attention and was surprised to see that the old man stopped at the edge of a small grass-covered clearing. On the far side he could see a blank face of rough sandstone rising almost sheer above the tops of a stand of pine trees.

'That there is called Fallen Rocks Cliff. It runs back up that ravine for most of a mile before topping out on a tabletop butte. Musta been a creek washing down at one time, but no more. Too rough to take a horse up and likely not much easier on foot. Now there's just a small creek over there, more like a seep. You can see there,' he pointed, 'where it weaves through the grass? We set up camp there when I was traveling with old Jim Bridger. I reckon we'll be comfortable. There's a kind of cave along there.'

The place they found was near perfect: a narrow opening in the rock wall, which had been washed out by a dried-up creek in the long past, gave them shelter. Looking over the little pocket of grass Con saw that the source of the little creek was a spring trickling out of the cave. It had been used by men before in the past; water filled a shallow basin at the mouth of the cave which somehow didn't look to be natural, before flowing on. The back of the cave was dark, but when the young man explored it he found it only went back a dozen feet or so before ending in a near-smooth rock face. The shallow cave, he thought, would give cover from any spring rainstorm. The horses were hobbled out on the grass.

'See that black soot up that wall?' Newell asked, 'there, near the entrance. I figure this place has been used by men for hundreds of years. It's got everything you'd need, firewood, water, protection and it's pretty well hidden. You tramp around these mountains and if you keep your eyes open you'll come across other good camping places too. Them people who was here before white man come along might have been savages but that don't mean they weren't smart.'

While Kincade rustled up firewood, Newell dug a hole in the sod back against the sandstone next to the cave mouth and built a small fire. They were using dry wood: what little smoke rose from the flames fanned out against the cliff face and quickly disappeared. After letting the coffee pot come to a boil and pouring their tin cups full, he sloshed the pot out and filled it with water.

'I don't know exactly what it does,' he said, using his belt knife to scrape the bark off a couple willow switches he'd gathered, 'but I recall Bridger making a poultice out of willow bark once when one of the trappers cut himself. The best beaver is taken in the first part of winter, you know. That's when the fur is prime. Up here in the tall mountains that means working in water that's usually froze over. That fella what cut hisself was so cold he didn't even know he'd done it until his hand started thawing. Bled like a stuck hog then, I'll tell you.'

After boiling the bark in the pot the old man mashed it into a pulpy mat which he placed over the holes in Con's arm. That doctoring hurt nearly as much as when he got the wound in the first place, but Con tried not to let on. Using the same pieces of cloth Newell tied the mess tightly in place.

'That'll do for a while. We'll keep an eye on it to make sure it doesn't poison up. Getting it clean is the best thing, I reckon. That poultice will take some of the soreness off, you mark my words.'

They were careful with their fire and put it out as soon as possible. Then they settled in for the night. No one said anything but all slept lightly and were wide awake long before daybreak. Munching on cold strips of smoked venison, the last of the fifty-pound supply they'd bought back at the fort, they waited for full light before moving.

'This is a likely place to hunker down,' Newell said. 'We don't move around much there won't be enough sign for any stray Indian to find. I reckon the first thing to do is for us to go take a careful look around.' He went on chewing on the same piece of rock-hard meat for what seemed like a long time. Almost indestructible, it was impossible to say when that poor animal had been killed and hung out over a fire to cure. A man had to work it patiently to soften it up for swallowing.

'That shoulder of yourn is going to take some time healing. It'll be faster if'n you weren't to move around. Kincade, what say we leave the horses here and scout out the surrounding area?' He took a stick and smoothed off a bit of bare ground. Then he marked a wavy line and put a small x below it. 'We're about halfway up a long, sloping ridge and if you were to cut down toward the bottom you might find some sign out on the flats. Me, I reckon I'll backtrack and try to find out where them redskins got to.'

Left alone, Con settled down with his back to a tree, hidden by the willows. Moving as little as possible, he scanned the little meadow and what he could see of the area around it. Newell and Kincade had hobbled the horses, which could be seen making the most of the wild grass. He made himself as comfortable as he could and rested, trying to ignore the pulsating of his wound. Relaxed, the dull drumbeat of hurt faded, becoming the background for his dreams.

The sun, moving across the empty blue sky, reached his upturned face and woke him up. Remembering where he was, he jerked awake. The tiny basin was still in the late-morning sunshine, a soft breeze bending the seed-heavy tops of the grass. The horses, standing with their heads down in the shade of the pines across the way, looked to be dozing. Vowing to stay awake, Con moved a little to get out of the direct sun and back into the safety of the tree's shadows.

Shortly before the sun dropped behind the ridge behind their campsite Newell stepped out of the trees. Circling around so as not to leave a trail in the tall grass, he approached the spring.

30

'Awfully quiet, old-timer,' Con called softly from the tree he had rested against all day. 'I hope that means that mean-looking Indian is gone?'

'Yeah, I reckon.' Newell nodded. He rested his Henry against a log and hunkered down. 'Kincade back yet?' Con shook his head and Newell went on: 'I found quite a sight of blood back where they ambushed us. Was two of them, from the sign they left. My guess is it was Blackhand and one of the braves we seen passing by. The shot took one of them, that's certain. The other helped the wounded one away. Found where they had left their horses. Prints show them leaving out of here.'

'Wonder where the others are? I didn't get a count but somewhere there's the rest of the bunch riding around.'

'Yep, they was hunting deer. I backtracked and found where they had set up a stand overlooking a pretty popular deer trail. Saw some blood where at least one animal was hung up and bled out. The horse sign all headed south from there, out toward the flat lands. I'd say that hunting party had gone out to make meat, got their animal and went back to the band.' Newell got up and started toward the fire pit, then stopped and grabbed for his rifle.

'Hey,' Kincade called from over near where the horses were standing, 'don't go getting hasty about putting holes in me.'

Newell laughed softly in relief. He leaned his

Henry back against the log, bent to poke the morning fire and, blowing on the few coals still smoldering, soon had a tiny blaze going. He filled the coffee pot and settled back to wait for it to boil.

'What'd you find?' he asked as Kincade, after checking over the animals, came into the camp. Con waved, using his right hand, and his partner smiled back.

'Well, you guessed right. There's been a passel of them traveling down on the flats. Lot of horses going somewhere, some were pulling travois, others being ridden. Must have been a good-sized horse herd, 'cause the mess they made of things nearly wiped out any other sign. I'd say it was someone's entire village, young and old, heading south.'

He settled wearily until his back was against a large rock. Then he looked over at Con. 'How's that shoulder faring?'

'Aches to beat the band, but it seems cooler than this morning. I thought it was going to burn me when I woke up.'

'Yeah,' Newell said, dropping a handful of crushed coffee beans into the heating water, 'and that's good. Likely there was a touch of fever. That poultice musta done its work, stopping it. We'll look to it after I make up some supper.'

He poured cups of coffee, then refilled the pot and set it back on the fire. 'That's the last of the dried venison. I picked up some wild onions this morning and that should make a tasty stew but we'll have to make a kill tomorrow or we'll get a mite hungry.'

Later Newell removed the wrapping on Con's arm. He nodded his satisfaction. 'Hey, maybe I oughta go into the business. Both sides look nice and pink. I guess we'll let the air get to it. Likely help it heal some.'

The next few days settled into a quiet pattern, Newell and Kincade leaving camp early in the morning, scouting for sign of intruders while exploring some of the nearby streams for color. Newell had shot a doe and butchered the meat; after cutting some of it into strips he hung them over a rack of willow branches he'd leaned against the sandstone wall. A thick lean-to made of spruce branches and a small fire built in another dug pit made it into a smoker. Con spent the days tending the fire, keeping it burning low, topping it up with green cedar boughs. The meat, Newell said, would be real tasty after a while.

As the days passed, Con became more active. He supported his left arm by sticking a thumb in his belt; his wound first scabbed over, then began to heal. His arm still hurt when he moved it, but it was better.

With the meat cured, there was little for him to do, so he started ranging the slope below the little meadow. Careful not to leave any sign of his passage and staying off any game trails, he hiked down and dropped into the next little valley. It was more of a narrow gully than a real valley, a yard-wide stream, both banks choked with willows, wound its way in a serpentine manner along its narrow floor.

Looking down, he studied the brush. It was a perfect place for deer to lay up through the heat of the day. The doe that Newell had shot was almost gone and another would have to be brought in. Slowly, and moving as silently as he could, Con eared back the hammer of his Henry and crept on up the creek.

When he came to the water's edge he stood still and looked around. Nothing moved.

'Probably just as well,' he muttered out loud. 'Don't know if I could carry a carcass back to camp anyhow.'

As he knelt to drink something in the water caught his eye. It was not the brown or wet gray of the surrounding gravel, or even like the little pieces of white quartz that sparkled through the water in the sunlight. He knew exactly what it was . . . gold. A tiny gold nugget.

CHAPTER THREE

Blackhand stood looking out over the prairie. He vowed he would be strong and not give in. To look at Spotted Tail, he felt, would be showing weakness, showing he knew he had been wrong.

'A leader of even a small hunting party does not wander away on a personal search.' Spotted Tail was not only the band's leader, he was one of the tribe's war chiefs. He was a man you did not argue with. There was little that Blackhand could say, but he said it anyway.

'It was white men in the sacred mountains. Letting them remain was to betray our honor.' Trying not to make his words a plea, he glanced at the older man's eyes. Catching himself, he quickly looked back over the plains.

'Lives in the Woods, or Ahahy as he is called, is unable to ride because of the white man's bullet. The band needed meat. Leaving the search to inexperienced hunters was a mistake. Mahpee is learning to be a good hunter and will prove himself when we begin the buffalo hunt but he is not a leader of men. Honovi and the others had to have someone to show them how. Mahpee could not. That was your job.'

The rebuke was strong and cut deep. There was nothing Blackhand could say.

'Yes,' Spotted Tail went on, almost sadly, 'the white eyes are unwelcome and can not be allowed to pass through, but the band comes first. I am told the young hunters let excitement cloud their judgement. Only one carcass was brought back into camp.'

Blackhand continued to stare out over the miles of grass, which was blowing in gentle waves in the afternoon sun. Shadows fled over the sun-browned grassland as huge gray-white clouds scudded across the pale-blue sky. A change in the weather was coming. The first hunt for the buffalo herd would have to wait another day.

'The band will join with Dull Knife's band of Cheyenne soon and the hunt will start. Until then I suggest you make yourself ready.' Spotted Tail stood for a moment, then walked away.

Blackhand seethed with shame. It was not right. The unspoken law was to keep the *Paha Sapa*, the sacred land, free of outsiders. The white eyes would have to be killed. Only then would the shame be removed.

*

Con hadn't brought a pan or shovel with him but with painstaking care and the blade of his belt knife he was eventually able to pick the piece of yellow metal out of the stream bed.

'Where there is one little bit,' he told Newell later, 'there could easily be more.' Kincade nodded his head in agreement.

The next day the three men returned to the ravine and explored. Panning here and there along the creek they ended up at sundown with a small amount of gold, enough to rattle around in one of the tin coffee cups.

For the next two or three weeks the men, using pans and a short-handled shovel, were able to half-fill the little cloth bag that had held coffee with nuggets and dust. They had run out of coffee at about the same time as the last of the flour and sugar was used.

In the excitement of their find, the days were spent working the gravels of the stream. Working from can-see to can't-see the three men slowly separated the heavy gold from most of the sand. The method they used was simple; one man used the shovel to fill the pan and the other two took turns swirling the pan, slowly letting the lighter material wash away. It was tiring work and on the third or fourth morning Newell said he thought

37

he'd better go take a long look around. They were getting low on meat again.

'We've been pretty lucky, I'd say. 'Course, there's no way of knowing, our heads've been stuck pretty close to that creek over there. But I reckon it'd be good to see if they's been anyone hunting us.'

'You go looking for Indians,' said Kincade. 'You know better'n me what to look for. I'll go on up over the ridge some and see about meat. Be a lot easier packing it back downhill than anything else.'

Con felt a little left out, but only nodded. 'It surely wouldn't do us any good to be filling every bag and sack we got with gold only to have some Indians come creeping up and getting nasty. You go get meat, take a look around and I'll keep digging and panning.'

Kincade was only gone a few hours when he came ambling back through the trees with a fat little deer carcass hanging over a shoulder. 'Now that wasn't so hard. The blamed thing just stood there looking at me, almost like it had nothing better to do than feed three hungry men.'

He hung the carcass up and proceeded to skin it out and cut some of the meat into strips. 'Con, I don't want to complain, but I'm getting mighty tired of cured venison. It's been so long since I tasted good beef, why I reckon I nearly forgot how it tasted.'

The younger man laughed. 'And fresh venison, good as it is, can't take the place of a cup of coffee. We're going to have to do something about that, I figure.'

He wasn't feeling too bad, though. During the day he'd come across a nice little pocket of gold that had sunk below the creek gravel and into a crack in the bedrock.

Newell returned at dusk with a big smile on his face and another deer slung over a shoulder.

'Not a sign of anyone anywhere. I went back to where we first saw them and then on down to that meadow they hunted. That's where I got this young buck. Ain't much to him, really, but what there is will cook up nice and tender. And looky here,' he went on, pulling a mass of dirt-covered tubers from a pocket, 'I found a bunch of camas root. You ever had any?' Seeing the others shake their heads his smile grew. 'Boy, you fellas got a treat coming. Clean them up and stick them in the coals to cook and they is something. We're going to feast tonight.'

They worked the creek another day before deciding to go exploring again. This time it was Newell who came into camp to describe a series of likely creeks.

'When we came here, to this camp, if you recall we came in over that ridge yonder,' he said, pointing back over a shoulder. 'Now if'n you was to

follow this dribble of a stream out, you'd be heading east and a little bit north. About a mile on, I'd
say, it flows into a pretty good-sized pond, almost a
lake. There's a small river what flows into it over to
one side and then continues on south. I'd say that
river would offer up some color, it's wild and with
the winter run-off it runs high and fast. Likely it's
way too big to work but the gravels along the way
might give up some color. My guess is that all along
that river are creeks coming out of the high country. Each one of them might be worth a good look.
I figure we could move our camp over that way and
work along the river. What do you say?'

After a few days' searching along that fast-
running river, with water flowing high with spring
run-off, they found their next bit of color. Digging
the gravels and sandbars was a lot harder work
though, and the amount of gold nuggets and
finds, what Kincade called the dust-and-gold-filled
sands, wasn't worth it. The old coffee-bean sack
was just a bit more than half-full.

Con's arm was nearly healed up, leaving flesh-
colored puckered scars on each side, but no more
pain. As they worked their way upstream, stopping
to prospect each creek that flowed into the faster,
wider water, he noticed Newell taking more and
more time off to go scout around and hunt. He
mentioned it to Kincade one afternoon and the
older man just smiled. It didn't come as a surprise

to either man when one morning the old-timer suggested it was time to return to Fort Laramie.

'Hell's bells, we been out of coffee for the best part of a month or more. No way can we go on eating nothing but deer meat and a few wild onions and the like. I reckon we could take the gold we got and go out, restock with grub and come back. Taking our time and being mighty careful we should be all right. Then we can really start working on filling some sacks.'

Con sat back and thought about it.

'No reason I can see for all of us to go,' he said at last. 'One person can travel as quick and as careful as three.'

Kincade slowly nodded his agreement. 'Newell, what say you take the gold and get what we'll need. Con and I'll stay up here and scout out likely streams to work. I've been noticing the water in this river has been dropping. I figure the winter run-off has all ran off. That might make it easier to find gold-carrying gravels, don't you think?'

Newell nodded. Con didn't think he was really paying attention. The old man wanted to go to town and that was what he was thinking about.

'But,' Con added, letting his words sound serious, 'you'll be carrying gold and you know what that means; there'll be those who'll want to know where you got it. Don't be letting anyone know where we are.'

41

'Naw, I'm smarter than that. I figure I'll traipse around and come in from the west, like I was maybe coming back from the Oregon diggings. If anybody asks, it's just some color I picked up west of the mountains.'

'How long you figure it'll take you?'

'Oh,' Newell looked off, thinking about where they were, 'I reckon a week or so to get far enough south and then a few days to sort out the supplies. I'll take my time coming back. Let's say, this time next month at the latest. It's coming on a full moon so start looking for me when the next one comes along.'

'All right. We'll meet here?'

'I'd rather we met back up there in that little pocket of grass we first stopped at by the Falling Rocks Cliff. Just in case I pick up some nosy redskins, it'll be a good place to hide out while we make sure we're all alone.'

'Sounds good. You be careful and we'll meet in a month or so.'

When Newell, after looking back to wave, disappeared in the forest downstream from their latest camp, for the first time in a long time Kincade and Con were alone. They didn't know it would be more than two months before either of them talked to a white man again.

CHAPTER FOUR

Newell took great care, riding south an extra day in order to come into the fort from the south-west. He carried little; his bedroll was tied to the back of his saddle along with a small leather bag containing his possibles, a small tin pot and a few other necessary items hung from his belt. The Henry rifle never left his right hand like it was almost a permanent part of him. Tucked into his worn leather belt was an old Smith & Wesson Army revolver. Kincade had once questioned whether it would even fire. The old man had to agree, it didn't look like it was worth much, the barrel was rusted and badly pitted. But, like the rifle, the pistol had been carried for a long time and he knew how to use it, if he had to.

Getting heavier as each day's ride began, and buried under every thing in his possibles bag was the coffee sack half filled with gold. It worried him some, packing raw gold. That, he decided, would be the first thing to take care of, changing the gold into real money. Not any of that Confederate scrip, either, but real Yankee gold coin.

The gold was worth more money than he'd ever had at any one time. True, it wasn't all his; most of it belonged to young Con and Kincade. But it didn't hurt to dream about what it'd buy, did it? No.

Thinking about the gold as he rode, he tried to recall the last time he'd had more than two coins to rub together. That thought brought a smile to his weather-creased face. He remembered. It had been at the end of his last trapping season two years or so back. He let his lips frame a smile as he thought about going up to the Green River rendezvous to sell his furs. Trapping was about over, the market for prime beaver was down and little cash money changed hands. Newell chuckled at the memory of selling his traps to a young greenhorn.

'Yep,' Newell had put all the pride he could in his voice. 'Bringing in a bale of prime beaver pelts is the work of a mountain man.' The youngster, he saw, had stars in his eyes. He was too late, the day of the wild mountain man was over. The youngster didn't know that, though.

' 'Course, I purely hate to let all this go,' he'd gone on, trying to look sad. The tenderfoot didn't notice, he was too busy inspecting the metal traps. 'But you see, I've got a niece who's been wanting me to come East. Says I'd better make the trip before I freeze up or some Injun pulls my hair. Wagh! Shows what she knows.' Newell had hesitated, spitting a stream of tobacco juice to one side and taking a quick glance at the young man standing there with a trap in his hands. He didn't want to overdo it.

'Howsomever, I figure it's about time. I 'spect I wait too much longer she'll forget who I am and I'll have to introduce myself to her. You understand, I reckon.' The young greenhorn couldn't take his eyes off the pile of traps and didn't look up, just nodding his agreement.

Newell set his price and let the buyer bargain him down a little before shaking on the deal. Both men thought they got the best of it. Newell was packed up and riding out of the rendezvous before daylight the next day.

Actually, he did have a niece back East and he did send some of the money to her. Margaret Baldwin was her name; she was his sister Irene's daughter. As a young girl, after Irene and her husband had been killed in an Indian raid, he had sent the young girl back East to a distant relative. She'd only been a sprig of a girl and Newell didn't know what else to do with her. He couldn't take her into the mountains after beaver, could he?

Every time he had a good year he made sure some of the trade was in gold coin which he sent East. Well, there was no reason he couldn't do the same this time.

The best thing to do, he thought, was to get shot of the gold. Walking into the Sutler's Saloon with a poke filled with gold was a sure-fire way to get into trouble. The only person in town capable of taking it off his hands was Harvey, the owner of the post's general store. He'd weigh it out and exchange it for coin, keeping a percentage for himself, of course.

He stopped off at the livery stable to treat his horse to a bait of oats and get the stable hand to rub the animal down. Then he walked down the wide dirt street to the store.

'Well, looks like you hit it big. Prospecting, were you?' the shopkeeper said, carefully weighing the gold on his balance scales.

Newell didn't want to say too much. 'Naw. I been carrying that since I left the Oregon country. Found a little bit here and there over on the other side of the mountains but didn't have no need to cash out. Now I do. Gonna send some of it back East to my niece.'

With a pocket full of twenty-dollar gold coins, Newell stood on the boardwalk and looked up and down the street. Yep, it was good to be back in civilization. No Indians shooting at him and a saloon

46

full of thirst-quenching liquor over across the way.

He nodded and set a beeline for the swinging doors.

The first glass of beer went down in two long swallows and, he thought as he signaled for a refill, merely washed away the dust caking his throat.

'Now, that's what this place has been missing. Old Angus Newell bending his elbow.'

Newell stopped with the second beer halfway to his lips to see his friend, Sheriff D.B. Taylor coming through the doorway.

'We've been missing you, old-timer,' the pear-shaped man said. Taylor had been carrying the sheriff's badge since the fort's commanding officer decided there was need for law in the growing community. Taylor was thought to be the ideal choice. He was a gentle man, and always had a good word to say to everyone, even those who got to spend the night in his jail sobering up. 'Someone said you'd gone back to trapping.'

Newell smiled, shook his head and sipped at his beer. 'Nope. Just took a little ride out to see what some of the rest of the world looks like.'

Taylor was a short, round man, with a waist wider than his shoulders. At first a person would think he was bald but looking closer you could see the pink skin on his head shining through the tendrils of thin hair so white as to almost be invisible. His round face, in keeping with the rest of

47

him, bottomed out at his pointy chin, which was almost hidden behind heavy jowls.

Sheriff Taylor motioned to the bartender for a beer and chuckled. 'And I'll bet a plugged nickel against a bucket of rain you found it ain't much different from what it was.'

'Oh, I don't know about that. Guess it all depends on your way of looking at things. Here, let me buy you that beer,' Newell said, digging into his pocket and pulling out some coins.

'Well, now,' Taylor said, seeing the Yankee double eagles, 'looks like I'd better check my Wanted posters to see if there's been any hold-ups lately. Thank you,' he added, taking a swallow of beer.

The sheriff wasn't the only one noticing the gold coins Newell had. Bart Starkey, standing a few feet down the mahogany bar from the two men, had been nursing his beer, trying to come up with a plan. He had arrived in town a few days before with less than ten dollars in his pocket and no prospects. He had put his last few coins down on the bar to pay for the beer and was only half-listening when the lawman came in. Bart Starkey was the kind of man who instinctively knew when the law was close by.

'No, sir,' Newell was telling the sheriff, 'this is honest money, the kind a fella has to work for. I got me a couple o' partners and, well, we worked mighty hard to fill this pocket.'

'And your partners let you alone with money, in the saloon? They must not know you.'

'Oh, I figure they do. I'm only having a couple glasses of beer before going over to Harvey's to pick up some supplies. This is the first drink I've had in, well, a month or more, I reckon.'

Taylor chuckled. 'You, a month without a drink? Now that's something, it is. 'Course now that you mention it,' the sheriff said, looking Newell up and down, 'you don't look as if giving up drinking is the only thing you've done. When's the last time you had a bath?'

'Go on with you. Tease all you want.' Newell laughed. Looking down at his clothes, he frowned. 'But I reckon you're right. A change of clothes and a real bath in a tub might be a good idea.'

'Another good idea would be to put that gold some place safe. It won't last long some of these out-of-work cowboys see it.'

'Yeah. Likely there won't be much left once I finish buying out Harvey's store.'

'Well, I'm off,' Sheriff Taylor said, finishing his beer. 'Thanks for the drink. And be careful with your gold, now, ya hear?'

Newell had slowed down and still had half a glass of beer in front of him after the sheriff left. He put an elbow on the bar, leaned forward and thought about the gold coins. A bath might be a good thing, but first there was something else he could do. Smiling, he waved to the bartender.

'Hey, you got some paper and a pencil back there? I think I'll write a letter to my niece.' He'd ask the post commander to send the letter and some of the gold coins East to Margaret. The money would probably be a welcome present to the young girl.

Starkey kept an eye on the old man as he took the paper and his beer glass and moved to an empty table. He'd been in town long enough to know about the alley that ran alongside the general store. It'd be a good place to wait for the old fool.

CHAPTER FIVE

When Angus Newell left the saloon he didn't turn down the dusty street toward the store, he went the other way, toward the post headquarters. Starkey, watching from the boardwalk next to the shadow-filled alley, cursed.

Somehow, sending the letter and gold off to his niece made Newell feel good. He was smiling as he came back down the street a short time later. Nodding to himself, he decided to soak in a tub of hot water down at the Chinaman's laundry before starting his shopping spree. Buying supplies and a couple horses would likely take another day and that meant at least one night in a hotel bed. He could afford a room for himself, one he wouldn't have to share with anyone, and that'd be a real treat.

Starkey watched and, staying on the other side of the street, followed Newell. He stopped and frowned when the man went into the Chink's laundry, but remembering the sheriff's comment about a bath changed the frown to a smile. He ducked around behind the buildings and followed the high board fence that enclosed the yard behind the laundry.

Peering through a narrow opening in the fence, he watched as Newell came out to the tub of water. There were two large tubs, both filled with water heated by the laundry and separated by a canvas curtain, one for men and the other for women. Bart Starkey watched as Newell undressed, hanging his clothes on a hook, and slowly eased his pasty white body into the steaming tub. Settling back, Newell closed his eyes and relaxed in the wet heat.

Starkey picked carefully at the lock holding down the latch on the gate in the fence and was inside the yard in a few minutes. Quietly making his way around and keeping close to the inside of the fence, he moved until he was standing next to the tub, directly behind the old man. Starkey's smile turned nasty as he brought the barrel of his six-gun down on the relaxed man's head.

Quickly he snatched the man's pants from the hook and ran out the back gate slamming it shut behind him.

Kwang Tung had been troubled by kids breaking into the bathing enclosure and when he heard the gate slam he rushed out from the laundry. Not seeing what he expected, he stopped and looked around. In the tub he saw the top of a man's head, a bloody gash turning the water pink.

Yelling for his helper, he reached in and pulled the white man's body from the water.

'Quick. Go for the sheriff. We must not let this man die here or we will be blamed,' he ordered. While the other man ran out into the street, Kwang Tung wrapped the old man in dingy towels he'd taken from a pile by the door. The man was breathing but was unconscious. Close to panicking, the Chinese laundryman looked around for a way to get rid of the body. It wouldn't be good for business to have him found dead here.

Before he could make a decision the sheriff came running through the laundry.

'What the hell's happened here,' the lawman demanded, speaking loudly so the Chinese man could understand. 'What've you done?'

Bending down, he saw that Newell had been bashed. 'Where's his clothes?' he asked, remembering the gold coins. Kwang Tung, his face looking almost greenish-yellow in fright, shook his head, then looking around, pointed to the shirt hanging from a hook.

'There, maybe.'

'Ah, hell,' Sheriff Taylor mumbled, 'whoever did this took the pants and the money. Damn it all to hell.'

He bent over Newell and gently lifted the old man's head to look at the wound. Newell's eyes fluttered and he moaned.

'What happened,' Sheriff Taylor asked quickly.

'Wrote a letter and sent her some money,' Newell said weakly. 'Don't want her growing up here, better for her back East.' As he looked up at the sheriff his eyes widened and then closed.

'Damn, he's dead.'

Among other things, Bart Starkey was a good listener. As he changed the handful of gold coins from the old man's worn pants pocket to his own, he began to feel like a new man. The first thing was to get rid of his worn-out clothes. A new pair of boots and even a new Stetson would help with that. As a young man, back before leaving New York for the California gold-fields, he had noticed that it was the well-dressed man who got the best service. Porters held doors open for a man in a pressed and brushed suit, while the everyday working man in his wool pants and shirt was left to fend for himself. Bart Starkey liked to be fawned over.

With money to spend, the next few days were pleasant for the murderer. After enjoying a good meal one late afternoon, he sat on the hotel porch smoking a cigar and listened to the latest gossip. Sheriff Taylor had about given up any hope of finding who had killed old Angus Newell.

'It seems that Newell had exchanged a poke of water-washed gold and had a pocket full of gold coins,' one man offered. 'D.B. is having all the shop-owners keep an eye out for anyone spending more'n they normally do.'

'Hell's fire, Yankee gold is the only money any of us got, leastways since nobody'll take that Confederate scrip anymore. That means we're all suspects?'

'I dunno. But I guess there ain't much else he can do, is there?'

A third person, sitting with his chair leaned back, his heels up on the porch railing, added what he knew to the conversation. 'I heard tell that Newell had sent a pile of that money back East to his daughter. Didn't know he had any family.'

'Yeah, it was his niece he sent the money to. The sheriff says Newell did that whenever he had a little extra.'

Nothing was said for a while and Starkey was about to move on over to the saloon for a drink when someone mentioned the gold.

'Wonder where the old man found that placer gold in the first place. He told D.B. he'd picked it up over in the Oregon country, but I wonder. I seem to recall him and a couple strangers talking down at the livery a month or so ago. I believe the newcomers had came in on the stage.'

'Yeah, I saw them talking over at the Sutler's

Saloon. There was two of them, strangers. Just a-talking and then they up and disappeared for a while, then here comes Newell without them two and with gold in his pocket. Makes me wonder, it does.'

Until then Starkey hadn't thought about where the old man had got his money, but if there was gold involved, maybe what he'd traded for the coins hadn't been all there was. He settled back in his chair. The drink could wait.

He didn't learn any more that day and had almost forgotten about it until overhearing something the sheriff said a week or so later. Keeping in mind what he'd heard about the sheriff watching out for anyone spending money recklessly, Starkey had been careful. It was while looking over a pile of bright-colored cotton shirts at the general store that he heard the shopkeeper talking with the sheriff.

'So, you're expecting Angus Newell's niece to be coming in on the stage?'

On hearing the name Starkey moved around until he could hear better.

'Yep. I got a letter from her this morning. Says she's coming out in answer to her uncle's letter. You know, that was about the last thing the old man said. Something about having written to his niece and sending her some money. It was just before he died. I figured it was the hit on his head that had him talking crazy. Guess not.' Starkey glanced over to see the sheriff slowly shake his head. 'I don't know what she expects to find. Damn it all, I just wish I could tell her we'd caught the man who killed the old man.'

'Ain't no way you coulda done more'n you did, D.B. There's too many men coming and going through here. On top of that, don't overlook those soldiers over at the post. I tell you, there's some bad apples in that barrel. Too many of them that came running out West to get away from the war, men from both the north and south. There were a lot of deserters and what better place to hide but way out here. Enlist in the army and for a few years get yourself a uniform and three meals a day. I tell you, there's a lot of bad men hiding over there and any one of them could be the killer.'

Starkey let a smile flit across his face. Yeah, he thought, blame it on someone over at the post.

'When's she due in?' Harvey asked.

'Any day now. I guess I'll have to be ready.'

Starkey watched as the two men finished their conversation and the lawman left before taking a heavy cotton shirt, a black one, up to the counter. He paid for it, nodded and left. He'd have to give what he'd learned some thought. If the old man had sent the girl some money, maybe he'd also told her something about the gold-poke he'd

57

come into town with. As he walked over toward the saloon Bart Starkey smiled. Like the sheriff, he'd just have to be ready.

CHAPTER SIX

The first thing Con and Kincade did after their partner left was to go hunting. Carefully, as before, they cut into strips the meat of the deer that one of them had shot and let the meat hang over a small fire. While Newell was gone they planned on spending as much time as possible hiking further into the mountains, checking every stream for gold. The more area they could cover, they figured, the more successful they'd likely be. Not having to worry about food for those few weeks would help.

'Let's not get so gold-hungry that we forget about the Indians,' Kincade warned, Con thought, like a mother hen. Since he had been no more than a tadpole the older man had been watching out for him. Young Conroy had grown up under that protection and hadn't questioned, when the decision was made to leave the family spread, the

Double C, that Kincade had naturally rode along too. Now Kincade was extra cautious. Con knew he was a bit uncomfortable to be riding through country where some red-skinned devil could be hiding behind any tree.

Con didn't comment, but he never let the threat of running into Indians get very far from his thinking.

The two men prospected down the creek from the camp until they got to the pond that Newell had talked about. Con figured it covered about five acres. From where he sat his horse he could see across to where another stream flowed in, disappearing in the dark blue water. The creek, on the other hand, poured through a jumble of boulders before plummeting ten feet or so in a foamy waterfall into the pond.

'You know, that water looks pretty inviting.' He looked over at his riding partner. 'C'mon, Kincade, it's time we had us a bath.'

'I got no problem with that,' the older man said, pointing toward the river side of the body of water, 'but it'll be shallower over there. I never did take to water like this. Neither one of us ever learned to swim and it looks darned deep here around this waterfall. I'm for getting clean but I ain't about to drown doing it.'

Con laughed and reined his horse down and around close to the shallow side. He pulled off his boots, stripped off his shirt and pants, and decided it would be a good time to wash some of the trail dirt from his clothes too. Soon, with their clothes hanging from bushes to dry, the two men were waist-deep in the cold mountain water, splashing each other and playing like a couple of kids.

The next morning they started out, following the river upstream, stopping at every little creek that washed down to join it. With every little stream, they'd look for a likely gravel bar, dig down to bedrock and work the sands found there. Trying not to leave any indication of what they were doing, or even that they were there, they had attempted to hide their prospect holes. Scrapping the sand and gravel back into their test holes, they thought the natural wash of the river would help out.

Years earlier when Kincade had come back from the California gold country he came without any gold, but his journey hadn't been wasted. He'd learned a lot in the time he was there. Gold was heavy and, while winter floods could push it along, it always worked its way through the sand and gravels when it could. Knowing how nature worked helped him in finding the best places to do their digging. Working along a number of streams, the two men dug and panned but found only a few flecks of the yellow metal.

One creek offered up a little more than any of

the others, so after carefully filling in the hole in the gravel they'd made, they turned up away from the river and followed its meandering course.

The creek they had decided to investigate ran through a gully that quickly got steeper and narrower. Soon, with the water flowing over huge boulders in white cascading falls they had to turn back. It was impossible to continue riding upstream.

That night they made camp on the far side of a bare rocky hill. In some far distant past, an upheaval had left house-sized boulders strewn everywhere. Finding a cavelike area big enough to hold the horses and to set up camp was easy. There was even a small spring that someone at some time had channeled into a rock basin. Just like the camp back at the little meadow, one far wall here was smoke-blackened and a pile of bone-dry firewood was stacked nearby.

'Wonder how long that woodpile has been there?' Con asked as he put together enough wood for a small fire.

'You know, it's getting late enough in the month that we ought to be heading back to meet up with Angus.'

Kincade chuckled softly. 'You sure it isn't that you're tired of deer meat for another meal?'

'That's probably got something to do with it. But it is getting towards the full moon. I reckon it's about time we went in that direction. If I got to eat venison I will and not complain too much but if there's a chance for real food, then I'd rather go get it. Ah, old friend, thinking about how good a cup of coffee will taste only makes it better.'

They didn't go back the same way they'd come up but cut over one ridge after another in a more straight line. Staying off the game trails as Newell had taught them, the two cowboys moved as swiftly and quietly as they could. By following a more direct route and not taking time to check out every little creek and tributary, they were making good time but were almost out of meat. One night they ate the last piece of dried deer meat for supper. The next morning, while Kincade was kneeling at a pool in the fast-moving water of yet another creek, he found gold.

Gold and Indians were the furthest thing from his mind at the time. He was paying close attention to a shadowed place next to a couple large rocks, thinking he might see a trout. Keeping his eyes open while sipping the cold water he saw something else. One of the pieces of gravel at the bottommost part of the pool was different. Remembering how Con had found that first bit of gold Kincade felt his heart start thumping. Moving slowly, so as not to disturb the water, he was able to pick the piece up. It was a nugget about the size of the lead of a bullet. Smooth from being washed by the water, but heavy; it was gold.

'Hey, Con. Take a look at what I found,' he called out, not taking his eyes off the nugget.

Con had saddled both horses and was bent over, checking the shoes of one. Riding the rough trails was wearing all the iron shoes down, he saw, and he was trying to figure how to deal with that when Kincade shouted. On looking up, he saw his friend peering intently into something in his hand. Seeing the look on his face Con smiled, knowing what it was. There was just something about gold, he'd learned, that made a man's eyes sparkle.

'I thought you were looking for breakfast,' he said with a laugh, walking over to stand next to the older man.

'Yeah, well if we were back in town right now, this little nugget would buy us the biggest and best breakfast that could be had.'

'Uh huh,' Con mumbled, poking at the yellow metal with a finger, 'but we aren't anywhere near a restaurant. Sure looks nice, doesn't it?'

'And I reckon if there's something like this here, there's got to be more right close by.'

For the rest of the day they worked the creek, finding not only gold but, even better, trout. As the split fish roasted over a small fire that evening, they took turns looking at the day's find. One of the tin coffee cups held grains and nuggets of gold. None was larger than the first one, but the cup was half-filled. With their stomachs stuffed with trout the two men felt happy and content as they rolled into their blankets.

Working their way upstream the next morning, they stopped at every bend in the creek for long enough to dig down into the gravels and, using the pan, wash out sand and rocks. By the end of the second day they figured there was almost as much in the tin cup as Newell had taken into Fort Laramie. Not only had they been finding gold, they had also caught more trout and found a huge jungle of blackberry vines heavy with ripe fruit.

Sitting by the fire that night, Con was carefully pouring their gold into a sack he'd made using the sleeve of an old shirt. Kincade, resting with his back against a log, looked up at the night sky.

'There it is, Con, our full moon. We've found a good place to work but it won't be going anywhere. What say we head out in the morning and ride back to that little meadow? Old Newell should be showing up and he'd be worried if we weren't there. The gold won't be going anywhere. It'll still be here when we get back.'

Hefting the makeshift sack, Con nodded. 'This here's at least double what we found in that other creek,' he said softly, holding the length of tied-off shirtsleeve, thinking that they were at last on the way to actually getting their ranch. 'But you're right. A good meal with real coffee comes next.'

As they came close to the meeting place they took their time and carefully scouted around, checking for any sign of Indians. They didn't find any but Kincade was able to shoot a deer which he bled out and then slung across his horse's shoulder just ahead of the saddle. Tired of venison though they were, it would be good to have more smoked meat for them to chew on when they headed back to the creek, which was now being called Gold Creek when they talked of it.

Back at the camp near the blank sandstone cliff, the deer meat hung from their makeshift smoke-house and the hobbled horses fed on the tall grass, the two men lazed around for a day or two, then spent a few days on foot, scouting the area.

Each morning, they woke up expecting to see the old man coming in, thinking about how good a cup of coffee would taste. Each night they went to sleep speculating on where their partner was.

'I wonder what could have happened.' Con broke the silence one evening after yet another meal of venison stew, this one thickened with several pieces of wild onion he'd found.

Kincade frowned, looking deep into the embers left from their fire.

'The full moon is a week or so gone. I've come up with a lot of things that could have happened.'

'Gawd,' Con said nervously, 'I damn well hope Angus didn't spend too much time in the saloon and forget why he was at the fort.'

Once that thought settled in, it didn't take long for the young man to decide that that was what had happened.

'I should have known it'd happen. Think back, Kincade,' he said a little later, 'that's where we met him, getting mighty close to drunk. Damn, now what'll we do?'

Sitting with his back to a tree through that afternoon, Kincade thought about it. 'I figure there are two things we can do. Head out toward Fort Laramie or go back to Gold Creek. Sooner or later we'll have to go into the fort, we can't live on a few wild onions, some berries and deer meat much longer. It'd be good, though, to be taking more gold with us when we do head out of the mountains.'

For another day they talked about it, arguing back and forth. At last they made the decision. On a piece of bark taken from an old pine snag and using charcoal Con wrote WAIT in big black letters and propped it next to the spring. Then they picked up their camp gear, put the cloth sack of gold in the bottom of one of the saddle-bags with the smoked meat on top, and headed back to the waiting gold.

Summer had been good for The People. Many buffalo hides were pegged out around the camp shared by Spotted Tail's Lakota Sioux and Dull Knife's Cheyenne. Each day the women of the bands would work the hides with their scraping knives, the first step in curing them. Meat hung high enough from racks throughout the camp to keep it out of reach of any camp dogs. It would be a good winter for The People.

It was a time for Blackhand and many of the other young men to learn, either by taking part in the hunting of the big beasts or by listening to the talk around the fires in the evenings. It was a time of plenty and nearly everyone was happy. Everyone except Blackhand.

Like a knife cut that wouldn't heal but festered, he still felt the anger behind the look on Spotted Tail's face when they talked about the failed deer hunt. The white men were the cause of it and because it was a time to make meat for the tribe, nothing had been done about it.

Not able to stand it any longer, Blackhand waited until dark one night and stole out of camp, leading his favorite buckskin pony. Taking the horse from the herd and working his way past the sleepy eyes of the young boys given the job of keeping the herd together was easy. Walking along, leading his horse, he was a mile or more away before pulling himself on to the buckskin's back.

Riding by the light of the full moon he made good time and when the sun first began to lighten the sky he was near where the trail to the hunting meadow branched off. Throughout the morning he rode the main trail, keeping one eye on the ground ahead and the other on lookout for any enemy.

Coming across any Indian in these sacred hills wasn't a worry; it was the white men he had to watch out for. Since before anyone's memory, this had been a place where all Indians honored the land. Enemies often met face to face here only to ride on without anger or bloodshed. What made it sacred for the Sioux was the belief that within this land was found the center of the world. All roads to the spirit world flowed through these mountains. This made it hallowed ground, not to be violated by white men who, everyone knew, believed in nothing.

When he stopped to water his horse at the little river some distance above a small lake, Blackhand saw where someone had been digging. No animal would dig there; it had to be man and that meant only a white man. Anger filled his chest as he jerked the single braided leather rein tied to the buckskin's lower jaw and kicked the animal into a run. Further upstream, where a small creek flowed in the river, he found more signs of digging. The white men were still here. They had to be found and killed.

But he could not hunt them down himself. That

was something that would have to be done by the men of the tribe. With this sign of digging, Blackhand thought, even Spotted Tail would have to agree. He turned the buckskin and headed back toward the prairie and the buffalo camp.

The great buffalo herd fed as they went, an enormous black wave of animals, moving at a steady, slow pace across the prairie. The hunters were careful not to excite the main herd, quietly separating the few they wanted from the others and then working with yard-long arrows and iron-tipped spears, bringing them down. It would take a lot of meat to supply the two bands in the coming winter months.

On coming back into camp Blackhand had rushed to make Spotted Tail aware of what he'd found. The young warrior was pleased to find the band's leader walking with Dull Knife of the Cheyenne. He waited until the two chiefs noticed him, then, after Spotted Tail nodded, he began:

'The whites are still trespassing. I found sign where they had dug into the bank, all along the little rushing river. This can not be let happen.' Stopping just short of making his words a demand, Blackhand looked his chief straight in the eye.

For a long moment nobody spoke. Spotted Tail looked deep into Blackhand's eyes, then turned to Dull Knife.

'This is Blackhand, son of my wife's brother,

Black Elk. We both have hopes that one day he will grow to be an important man of our tribe, possibly even a war chief. Now he still thinks like a young boy, however.' Blackhand's face flushed at the words. 'This young man must learn that everything will happen when it is time, that many things have to come together in their own way in order for the tribe and each band to continue.'

Turning to look at Blackhand again, Spotted Tail frowned. 'Once again you went off on your own when the people had meat to make, to be ready for life in the coming winter. Once again it is your hatred of the white men that led you to make this decision. Again I say to you, it is not yet the time to hunt the white men, it is time to prepare for the winter months. That is what I say, wait until the summer hunt is done before doing anything about them.' Without another word Spotted Tail turned away.

For a long moment Dull Knife looked into Blackhand's face before, with a single nod, he turned to catch up with the Sioux chief.

Blackhand was left standing alone, his face as black as his name with anger. Wait until the hunt was over. That meant sitting in camp or hunting with the other young men for two more moons, until the Moon of Grass Dying. He didn't want to wait that long. Watching the two men walk away he slapped a hand against his thigh; he would not wait that long.

With that oath to himself he started making his plans. Quietly over the next few days he laid out his ideas to a few of his closest friends, Howls at Night and Broken Nose. 'We can ride back into the sacred mountains and find where the white eyes went. Lives in the Woods has not been well since being shot. If we bring back the hair of his enemy, his spirit will heal.'

Howls at Night immediately nodded. He was a year younger than Blackhand, his small, slender body lacked the strength of the others. All his life he had had to prove to everyone how brave he was, even though he knew that he was always frightened. Afraid that if he didn't go along, Blackhand would think badly of him, he nodded his willingness to go.

Broken Nose was not so sure. 'Spotted Tail would not like us going off while there are buffalo to kill. He was unhappy with the last hunt you led, Blackhand. Who knows what he would do if we leave now?'

'I'll tell you what he'll do, Broken Nose: nothing. We will bring back the white men who are trespassing on our land, or at least their scalps and weapons. With that even Spotted Tail would have to welcome us as heroes.'

'I will think on it,' the more cautious Broken Nose mumbled, turning and walking away.

The other two watched him for a moment.

72

'He'll go with us. This is a chance to show we are worthy,' Blackhand muttered quietly. 'Soon it will be time to return north. Before then I want to take my spirit quest. With the white man's hair on my belt, the spirits will be happier with me.'

Howls at Night didn't respond. Feeling trapped, he knew that no matter what happened, it wouldn't be good for him.

'We'll wait to the next dark moon,' Blackhand decided, nodding to himself as he made the decision. 'Then we go after the white eyes.'

CHAPTER SEVEN

There were times when Margaret Baldwin was sure she hadn't made the right decision. When she paid her train fare, the clerk let his eyes flash up at the young woman before dropping quickly back to business. A young man who had never traveled farther west than his pa's farm on the outskirts of town, he was surprised to hear where she wanted to go. Mostly when he sold a ticket to end of track it was to drummers, men of questionable character or, once in a while, a family looking for land to settle on, not an attractive young woman. And she apparently was traveling alone. He didn't ask any questions.

If he, or anyone for that matter, had offered advice she might have given her decision another thought. But nobody did. Frowning, she gave her head a little shake. Stop fooling yourself, she chided herself silently, it wouldn't have made any difference. She didn't really have a choice.

Uncle Angus's letter with the hundred dollars had been a life-saver. It hadn't been the first time he'd sent money and each time it seemed to be just when she was in dire straits. Money hadn't been easy to come by, not while she was in school, but there had been enough so she got by quite nicely, thank you. It was after school ended that things got tough. The only work, it seemed, at least for a gentle lady, was as a nurse or a typewriter and she wasn't qualified for either of these.

For a brief time she considered returning to class to train as a nurse. That was when she discovered the education she had received, while excellent, wasn't considered suitable for a woman. Actually, when she presented herself to those in need of a clerk, they rarely even gave her the time of day.

Kicking a table leg in disgust, she let the frown grow. Men. For some reason it was only men who ran the banks and other companies and for that same reason they would only hire other men to manage their books. It was not fair.

Returning to school to become a nurse was out of the question. She didn't have the money. The same thing held true for those learning that new position, as an operator of that new machine, the typewriter. The money Uncle Angus sent wasn't enough to go back to class but it was enough to take her to Fort Laramie, with just a little left over, if she was thrifty.

The first doubts about her decision came when, sitting on the hard bench of the train station as she waited for her baggage to be loaded, one of the rough-looking men sat down beside her.

'Well, sister, if you're waiting for that train west then it looks as if we'll be traveling together. Might as well become friendly, don't you think? Make the trip go by faster.'

Margaret glanced at him and scooted to the far end of the bench. Not wanting to offend him, she fought back the urge to shiver. A big man, he was dressed in a worn wool suit that was shiny with ground-in dirt. He needed a haircut and a shave, and even with the distance between them she could still smell him.

'No, thank you. I prefer to keep to myself,' she murmured, turning to look away.

The man chuckled and moved closer to her. 'Now, missy, that ain't friendly and I am a very friendly kind of fellow.'

'The lady said no, Rufus. Didn't your mother ever teach you what that meant? Or did you have a mother.' Another man, almost equally rough-looking but with a clean-shaven chin, stood a few feet away with his hands on his hips, fingers only inches from a pair of holstered pistols.

'Now, damn it, Cole, I ain't doing nothing that's

76

any o' your business,' the dirty man complained, his words almost a whine.

'I reckon I'll make it my business, Rufus. Now go away. Fact is, smelling your stink is beginning to bother me something fierce. Why don't you and your friends over there go out on the platform to wait, leaving these good people in peace.'

Rufus stood up and looked directly at the other man. 'Cole, one of these times you're gonna push me too far.'

Cole laughed, but Margaret saw the laugh didn't reach the man's eyes. 'But this isn't that time, is it, Rufus? Now go wait outside.' He turned as Rufus shambled past him and watched as he motioned to the other men going out of the station.

'Don't be paying old Rufus any mind, ma'am,' Cole said, his voice softening and losing the hard edge it had had. 'I don't mean to be nosy, but I couldn't help but overhear you buying a ticket to end of track. Forgive me, but isn't that a mite, well, dangerous for a young gentlewoman such as yourself?'

'I can take care of myself, thank you,' Margaret responded; then, realizing how it sounded, she apologized. 'Oh, I am sorry. I shouldn't be like that, not after your helping me with that . . . that man.'

'Ma'am, there isn't a man in this waiting-room that wouldn't have come to your aid,' Cole said.

He motioned to the bench. 'Do you mind if I sit down a minute?'

'Oh, no sir, please do.' This man, she saw, was vastly different from the other, Rufus. For one thing his suit wasn't as worn-out and the shirt, mostly hidden by the suit coat and vest, looked clean. Well, she noticed, maybe it was a little gray around the collar.

'Do you realize Rufus is one of the kind of men you'll be running into once you leave the city? Not every one, but far too many of them. Again, begging your pardon, but are you ready for that?'

Margaret looked down at the toes of her buttoned-up shoes. 'No, not really, but,' glancing up let a smile twitch the corners of her lips, 'I'm afraid there isn't anything I can do about it. I'm traveling to Fort Laramie to meet with my uncle.'

'Fort Laramie. Whew, ma'am, now that *is* the end of track. Fact is, it's the end of nearly everything.'

'Have you been there?'

'Oh, yes, I have. Tell the truth, it's the army being there that caused me and the boys to make a visit. Was something about a payroll. That little trip didn't work out, however. The army was just a mite too awake and aware.' He smiled as he saw the young lady hadn't understood his meaning.

'What's it like? I know it's pretty far and there might be wild Indians and the like, but is it really like the newspapers say it is?'

'You had better believe it.' Wanting to change the subject, he asked about her uncle. 'I know a lot of men in that part of the country, maybe I've met up with your uncle. What's his name?'

'Angus Newell. He was a trapper and scout and . . . well, I don't know what all.'

'Angus Newell,' Cole mused. 'Yes, I did hear something about an old mountain man named Newell. A crusty old-timer, as I recall. Hmmm,' he said, running a finger along his lower lip. 'You know, I think he'd be a mite worried about you traveling out west like you're planning on doing. The train only goes so far and then it'll be a stage coach.'

'Yes, I'm aware of that. But, as I said, it's all I can do.'

'There are all kinds of people moving West, some looking for a new life and others just wanting to get away. Not all will want to take advantage of an attractive young woman but there'll be those that do.' He stopped and, looking down at her worried frown, smiled. 'There isn't much you can't handle yourself, though. Not if you've got the right tools.'

Margaret shook her head, not understanding.

'Two things you'll need, first is strength. Be strong and look them right in the eye. Most bad men are cowards and those kind don't like someone who can't be frightened. I can't help you with that, but the second thing I can.' Reaching into the right-hand pocket of his vest, he deftly flipped out a small derringer.

'This might help you if you really get in trouble. It's a fairly new Colt pocket pistol. Some folks call it a derringer, named for the fellow who invented it. I took it from another man who didn't have a need for it any more. Now don't think of it as a toy, it'll fire the same bullet as either of my belt guns. But there's only one bullet in this and it won't be much good unless what you're aiming at isn't mighty close. If you have to fire it, you had better make sure you hit what you're pointing at. Have you ever shot a pistol before?'

'Yes, as a girl my pa showed me how to hold one,' she said, taking the tiny weapon with two fingers. 'But I was very young and that was a long time ago.'

'Don't worry. If you feel the need to pull this out of your purse, being strong and pointing it at someone will usually make him back off. Nobody likes to have a gun pointing in their direction.'

'But I couldn't accept it as a gift and I certainly can't afford to pay you for it.'

Cole laughed. 'Go ahead and put it in your purse. When you get to Fort Laramie, you give it to your uncle and tell him where you got it. I'll get it back from him somewhere down the line.'

'You do know my uncle?'

'Not really. But there aren't that many grumpy old mountain men hanging around when you get out of the city. And don't worry about paying for it. The fellow I took it from isn't going to miss having it. He just wasn't strong enough, I'd say.'

Margaret opened the drawstrings of her cloth purse and dropped the pistol inside.

'All you have to do is pull that out, thumb back the hammer and point it. That'll change the mind of any one wanting to fool with you.'

For the next 200 miles or more nobody paid her any attention and she had almost forgotten the little pistol. She had other things to worry about. Although the seat she'd taken was leather-covered and had some padding, it was soon as uncomfortable as the hard wooden bench back at the station. The sleeper compartment she'd paid for wasn't much better and that car was left behind after the first night. From then to end of line, a small town somewhere in the Nebraska Territory, the passengers had to make do on the straight-backed seats.

The stage line that ran the next part of her trip West was running late and she had to stay overnight. Taking a room at the hotel was too expensive so she spent the long hours curled up on a cot in the ticket agent's office. The agent, being a kindly, balding man with stooped shoulders, let her stay there for only two dollars.

It was one of the passengers taking the stage who brought back Cole's advice.

'Well, missy,' said the tall cowboy sitting across from her, a big buck-toothed smile brightening his suntanned face, 'looks like it's just you and me all the way to Fort Laramie. Now, what say we get to know each other?'

Margaret thought his smile was friendly but didn't like the glint in his eyes. Frowning, she stared into his blue eyes and slowly pulled the derringer from her purse.

'No, I don't think that would be a good idea, especially in such a small place as this.'

Seeing the pistol pointed at his belt buckle, the cowboy raised both hands and let his smile fade. 'Whatever you say, ma'am, whatever you say, just don't go pointing that little thing at me no more.'

The rest of the journey was spent quietly; not comfortably, but quietly.

Fort Laramie wasn't what she expected. She'd talked to everyone she could who had any information about this part of the country, but she wasn't ready for the real thing. She knew the army post was the reason for the community and had anticipated having the military in more evidence. Stepping down from the stage into the thick dust of the dirt street she looked around and didn't see any indication that the army was anywhere near.

The steps up to the hotel porch the stage had stopped in front of were thick, rough-sawn planks. After her baggage had been placed, not too gently she thought, on the porch, all she could do was stand there, taking in the town.

People passing by, mostly men, stared at her. Finding a young woman all alone with a lost look on her face made them wonder.

'Ma'am,' a heavy voice behind her broke into her thoughts. 'Is there someone meeting you?'

Looking quickly around, and dropping a hand into her purse, she started to shake her head. When she saw the big, silver six-pointed star on the man's chest she relaxed a little and smiled.

'I . . . no, I guess not. I wrote my uncle but I couldn't tell him when I'd arrive.'

'I'm Sheriff D.B. Taylor, ma'am. Who is your uncle? Maybe I can help you find him.'

'Angus Newell, Sheriff,' she said, not noticing how the name caused the lawman's expression to change.

'Ah, I see.' He looked down the street so she wouldn't see his discomfiture. 'Well now. You'd be Angus Newell's niece then. Why don't we go down to my office? Get off the street to where we can talk without half the town trying to overhear. It seems,' he went on as he picked up her two suitcases and, not waiting, turned to walk down the broad plank sidewalk, 'that every time the stage gets in, half the town is there to see who's arrived. Nosiest people I've ever met, I swear.'

Trying to keep the young woman from asking any questions, he continued talking until they got to his office. He pushed through the door, motioned her to a chair and then sat behind his desk.

For a moment neither spoke. Then, clearing his throat, Sheriff Taylor started to explain. 'When your letter arrived, well, we didn't know what to do. So I opened it and read that you were coming. I wrote right back, but I guess you'd already left.'

'Why would you . . .' she started to ask, then stopped. 'Uncle Angus is dead?'

'I'm afraid so, ma'am. He apparently died the same day he sent you a letter.'

Margaret was stunned. What would she do now?

CHAPTER EIGHT

'How did he die?' she asked, not really thinking about that but feeling the need to say something.

'Well, it was a blow to the head that killed him. He had just got to town and after writing to you he went over to the Chinaman's for a bath. I'm sorry to tell you, but nobody saw anything. We don't know who killed him.'

'But why would they? From what he said in his letters, he was just an old man, a trapper.'

Taylor nodded. 'Yeah, he was pretty well known here in Fort Laramie. He had a little cabin just outside of town. Came in for a glass of beer and a game of pinochle every day or so, and to catch up on the gossip. Everybody liked him.'

'Then why kill him?'

'He didn't say much about it, but a month or so before his death he and a couple of men he had met rode out of town. A while later Newell came back with a poke of gold, traded it for coin over at the general store. I'd guess that's about when he wrote you. Next thing, he was found dead out back of the laundry where the Chinaman's got a couple of tubs. The gold coins that'd been in his pants was gone. We found his pants down the alley a piece. No sign of the coins, of course.'

'He told me a little about his partners. Uncle Angus said they had gone out into the Black Hills and were prospecting. They had found enough gold, he said, that he could send me some money. I was finished with school and wrote that I was coming out.'

'Yeah, your letter was left with me and I opened it. I wrote to you right away, telling you about your uncle's death, hoping to catch you before you left. It musta just missed you.'

For a long minute the two sat there, both deep in thought.

Margaret didn't cry, not for losing her only relative, a man she really didn't know, nor for the uncertainty of her future. Uncle Angus had already been buried, so there was no reason to mourn him. Not in public anyhow.

Eventually Sheriff Taylor broke the silence, asking the question she was asking herself.

'What will you be doing now? None of my business, of course, but, well, this is a pretty rough place for a young Eastern woman such as yourself.'

She could only think of one thing she could do. 'Tell me about these partners he had gone prospecting with. Uncle Angus didn't really tell me much about them. Do you know them?'

'Nope. A likely-looking young man and an older man, one person said. I think it was the bartender over at the Sutler's Saloon. Said they were cowboys by the look of them. They'd just come into town and met up with Angus and a few days later rode out. They was three of them rode out, as I said, and only Angus Newell rode back in. He did say he was going to be spending most of the money over at the store for supplies, so I reckon he was going back out, but I don't know, he was pretty cagey about it. Only natural, of course, when there's gold involved. Nobody knew who the strangers were and nobody's come in asking about Angus. 'Fraid there ain't much more I can tell you.'

'Well, I can't go back East, there's nothing there for me.' Suddenly she made up her mind. 'I suppose that only leaves one thing for me to do. I'm going to go look for my uncle's partners. They're my partners now, whether they know it or not.'

Sheriff Taylor didn't say anything, but slowly shook his head. 'Ma'am, you know best, but there's a lot of country up there and not many people. Them that are there will be Indians and they don't like it much when white folks come traipsing through.'

Margaret's frown didn't change. It didn't sound safe, but then what could she do? Going back East was out of the question, she didn't have enough money for that. Staying here would mean going to work in a restaurant or store, if any jobs were to be had. No. She'd have to do as that man, Cole, had said: be strong and look any trouble straight in the eye.

'Sheriff, I don't doubt you're right, but there's nothing else for me to do. Now, someone must know how to find my uncle's partners. I've got his letter and, well, just a little money. That's all. It'll have to do.'

Sheriff Taylor shook his head as he watched her walk across the dusty street toward the hotel.

Bart Starkey thought about what he'd heard and smiled. He'd been sitting on the hotel porch when the stage came in and had watched as the sheriff met the girl. Old D.B. had talked enough about waiting for Newell's niece to arrive, so that everybody knew who she was the minute she stepped down from the coach.

Following a little behind them, Starkey had taken a chair outside the sheriff's office, as close to the office window as he could, and leaned back against the wall. Whoever had built the jail hadn't wasted any more lumber than they had to; the walls were thin-sawn planks. It didn't take much to hear the conversation inside. If Newell and his

88

partners had found gold up in the Black Hills, then Starkey was interested. The girl, he thought, smiling, might be his ticket to that treasure. The old man must have said something in that letter he'd sent her. He'd have to think on it a little.

Blackhand was an angry young man. He chafed at being kept busy with the hunt. For days on end, the men had been killing buffalo. There were so many that Spotted Tail had ordered the men to help with the cutting of meat into strips. That, the young man thought, was woman's work. It was not suitable work for a man. Especially not when there was sign of white men trespassing in the *Paha Sapa*, the sacred mountains.

The shame he felt for the tongue-lashing he had received from Spotted Tail fed his resentment. No one said anything to him, but he knew his failure with the hunt was talked about. Bringing his wounded friend, Ahahy, into the camp turned out to be more sign of his inability to lead. Shamed, his fury grew every day that passed.

'Soon,' he told Howls at Night, 'the hunt will be finished. Then we will start our own hunt.'

Howls at Night was not happy about that. None of the other young men would even listen when Blackhand talked of hunting the white men. Not even when he called for revenge for Ahahy's injuries. Growing up together, Broken Nose,

Howls at Night and Blackhand had been close friends. Now not even Broken Nose would listen.

The two bands, Spotted Tail's Sioux and the smaller group of Cheyenne led by Dull Knife, had taken many of the big shaggy animals. Most of the meat had been sun-dried or smoked over slow-burning fires and was already packed away in parfleches made from the cured buffalo hides. Soon the decision to start the trek back north would be made but before that there would be a celebration in honor of another summer's successful hunt.

When talk of the coming event spread though the camps, Blackhand made his own decision. The hunt was close to being finished. Nobody would miss a few of the young men if they left camp. Making the rounds to those he thought would go along, he told them to check their bowstrings and sharpen their arrowheads. If the white men were still in the sacred mountains, they would soon die.

Con and Kincade once again took a roundabout direction and didn't ride directly back to Gold Creek. Without Newell leading the way, they were both feeling more alone all the time and very vulnerable. They rode with great caution. Keeping to faint game trails and at times simply traveling where there was no trail at all, they rode slowly, knowing a sharp-eyed Indian would have little trouble finding sign of their passing. By staying in the bushy upper ridges it was hoped that whatever tracks they were leaving behind would not be found by anyone.

'It's tough on these animals,' Kincade said once, scratching his horse's nose. They had pulled up to let their horses catch their wind. 'I took a look this morning at their shoes and let me tell you, they're starting to wear mighty thin.'

'I know. I've been keeping an eye on them myself. Way I got it figured, though, it's only another day's ride over to Gold Creek. I'd say we work that creek as long as our food lasts and then head out to Fort Laramie. We should have enough gold in our saddle-bags to stock a nice piece of ground by then. Taking our time riding out, and being careful, we should be all right.'

Kincade nodded. 'Well, hoss, you hear that? Another day or so of hard work and you'll get your chance to rest up.' Turning to look over his shoulder at their back trail, he mused. 'I think you've probably got it right, though. Anyway, I doubt any Indians will come looking for us up here in the high country.'

After riding on some way the next morning they stopped to water their mounts. Looking higher up at a snow-covered peak, Kincade smiled. 'You know, I think this might be your Gold Creek. That high peak up yonder is just about in the right place.'

'Well, that could very well be. Leastways it's a good place to start looking. Let's drop downstream and check it out as we go. If this isn't Gold Creek, then it's got to be close by.'

Over the past few weeks they had learned exactly what kind of place to watch for. Usually it was where the creek made a sharp bend that was most likely. The two men rode carefully downstream until they found what looked to fit the bill. A sweeping bend in the creek with a riffle of shallow water at the head of a pool looked to be a good place to set up camp. A huge boulder acted as a dam, forcing the creek to curve sharply and leaving a patch of thick-growing grasses in the elbow of flat land that the water curled around.

'Now, looky here, hoss,' Kincade told his horse as he stripped the saddle and bridle off. 'Didn't I tell you you'd get to rest? What do you think, Con? I reckon this is as good a place as any to set up camp. We can work on down the creek from here.'

The rest of the afternoon was spent cutting pine boughs for their bed and digging a fire pit, making camp as comfortable as possible. After hobbling the horses, Con started heating water in the old coffee pot. The pot had been used so many times to make venison stew, the easiest way to eat the dried meat, that it no longer even smelled of coffee.

'Boy, what I wouldn't give for a cup of good

camp coffee,' he said, letting the strips of meat soften in the hot water.

Looking out over the pool he thought he'd see if there were any fish in the quiet water. There had been worms in the dirt when he dug the fire pit and he had a long stretch of thin line and a hook or two in his pocket.

'What about trout for breakfast,' he asked Kincade, who had already settled with his back against a large boulder.

'Sounds mighty good. I think I'll just doze here a mite while you see how lucky you are.'

The water flowing into the pool struck the boulder and was pushed to the side, changing direction and continuing on. Standing knee-deep in the water with his baited hook sitting out on the bottom of the pool, he studied the rock. It might be worth looking into the base of that rock, he thought, then quickly forgot it when something jerked on the end of the fishing line.

What had looked to be a boulder turned out to be the face of a small rock shelf. Using a long tree-limb, the two men spent most of the next morning prying smaller rocks away from that shelf, changing the course of the creek. When they stopped to eat the rest of the cooked trout the water no longer pushed against the rock wall but now curved a few yards before it. Anything being forced down the creek by flooding water and stopped by the huge rock would be caught in the gravel that could be seen in the little pond left behind. It didn't take them long with the shovel and pan to realize they had found a rich pocket of gold.

Digging deeper and deeper into the gravel, they worked from morning sunrise to dark for another week or so, carefully emptying each day's heavy gold and the little amount of black sand left in the bottom of each pan into one pair of saddle-bags.

'We been here before, Con,' Kincade said after cleaning out the pot one evening, 'out of meat and still no coffee. I'd say it was about time we took a ride back out to the meadow.'

Con simply nodded. 'I've been thinking the same. There's enough gold in those saddle-bags to set us up, I'd say, wouldn't you? I know they're getting mighty heavy.' At the older man's nod, he went on. 'Yeah, I guess it's time. Go back and see if Angus has showed up and if not, then head for town. There's still a sight of gold to be found but we've got enough for our needs. No reason to be greedy.'

The next morning, Con's horse, its sides fat and smooth-skinned from days of doing nothing but feeding on the rich wild grass, put up a little ruckus when the saddle was cinched down. Con only laughed and stuck a knee in the animal's side.

He was a happy man; he knew that in his saddle-bags he had his ranch. He didn't have time to put up with a feisty horse.

CHAPTER NINE

Blackhand rode proud, his back straight as he left the band's camp, not letting his eyes look to either side. That, he thought, was how a leader of men should appear, and he was a leader. Instead of slinking away in the night with one or possibly two others, he was leading ten young men. With that following, not even Spotted Tail could call him back.

Both Howls at Night and Broken Nose had in the end agreed to help him find the white men and, when they were bragging about what they were planning, others, bored with the buffalo kill, nodded.

'Where will we begin looking for the white eyes?' Howls at Night asked, pushing his pony closer to Blackhand. Remembering how Ahahy had been shot, Howls at Night was not looking forward to the trip, but he could not find a way out of it.

Careful to take his time, Blackhand didn't look around. 'We will begin where we saw them before. Even now there will be sign of their passing. After all, they are clumsy whites.'

Blackhand didn't waver, he knew where he'd found the sign of someone digging in the little river and he headed directly for that place. Riding ahead, he was the first to see the spot. He turned to point it out, letting the others see where someone had been digging in the gravel near the water.

'It is too early for the white eyes to be trapping beaver,' Broken Nose said, standing beside Blackhand and looking down at the place. 'What would anyone dig for there?'

Blackhand didn't respond.

Riding higher into the mountain valley, they found where, at nearly every little creek, someone had dug into the sand and gravel.

The excitement of hunting white men faded as the party rode higher, but vanished like drops of water on a hot rock when all signs of digging disappeared. The trail was lost and Blackhand didn't know where to look.

As he sat on the back of his horse watching the animal drink, the young leader felt his stomach muscles knot. He'd been so sure they would find the trespassers. Turning back now would be the end of his standing as a warrior.

'Blackhand,' Howls at Night kept his voice low as he gigged his horse alongside. 'Which way do we go? Broken Nose and some of the others are talking about going back.' Speaking quickly he went on: 'It is not me who is saying these things. No one brought enough food for a long hunt and there are some who are not sure there will be white men to kill at the end of this ride.'

'Only white men would dig the gravel,' Blackhand growled. Could they not see it? 'We have missed where they left the river. We must turn back to pick up their trail again.'

Blackhand pulled his horse's head sharply around and beat his heels into the animal's side.

'Come,' he ordered, 'we will find the white eyes.'

'Excuse me, Miss Baldwin,' Bart Starkey let his smile light up his entire face. 'I couldn't help overhear you talking with Sheriff Taylor when you got off the stage. I wonder if I might have a moment of your time.'

Starkey had followed the young woman when she left the sheriff's office and had stopped her as she crossed the street and went up the steps to the hotel. Margaret stopped on the hotel porch and looked down at the big, broad-shouldered man who stood in the dirt of the street, holding his wide-brimmed hat with the fingers of both hands.

It had become her habit, when approached by any man, to let one hand slip into the top of her cloth purse. As she kept that hand and the purse in the folds of her skirt nobody could see she was holding the little pistol.

She looked the stranger over. She saw that, unlike most of the men she had seen since arriving in Fort Laramie, this one's chin was clean-shaven, his mustaches hanging down on either side of his full-lipped mouth. His hair, combed back from his high forehead and behind his ears was a mousy-brown color. There was something about his eyes that she wasn't comfortable with.

'I'm Bart Starkey, miss. I didn't mean to eaves-drop, but, well, everybody who knew Angus heard that his niece was coming. The sheriff didn't make any secret of it.'

'You knew my uncle?'

'Well ma'am, 'most everybody knew old Angus. I mean everyone who's been in these parts long.'

Margaret looked over her shoulder. She saw a scattering of rocking-chairs on the porch and motioned the man to take one, sitting herself in another.

'I didn't get to know him,' she said, letting her gaze drop to the toes of her shoes. The heavy wool traveling dress still had a covering of dust from the long stage ride. Feeling the grit that had settled on her since leaving the train only made her feel more depressed. A nice hot bath would make her feel better, she thought. 'When my parents were killed Uncle Angus sent me East to relatives. I was a young girl then and don't really remember much about him. Tell me, what kind of man was he?'

Starkey thought a moment. All he wanted was to get a hold of the letter. Maybe there would be something in that about the gold or the partners. He wasn't sure how far he could go, talking about a man he'd never met except when hitting him on the head.

'He was a lot like most old-timers, I'd say. Easy to get along with, liked to talk of things he'd seen and places he'd been. Like the Black Hills country.'

'Oh, you know about the Black Hills? Uncle Angus said in his letter that he and his partners had found gold. Sheriff Taylor said he was in town to buy supplies when he was murdered.'

'Not many men know much about the Black Hills. 'Most everybody coming West is heading for California or the Oregon Territory. But from what I've heard there might just be gold in other places.'

'Have you traveled through that area?'

Starkey ran a hand through his long hair and let a smile play across his face. 'Quite a bit of it, actually. I've been working as a scout for the army, trying to keep track of any Indians that might cause trouble. Those mountains are sacred to 'most all the tribes but with the army fort right here, they're pretty peaceable, for the most part.'

An army scout, Margaret thought. Maybe he'd know how to find Uncle Angus's partners. 'Mr Starkey, I'll be frank. I'm in quite a fix. Uncle Angus sent money East to me and, not knowing of his death, I spent nearly all of it coming out here. He wrote in his letter about him and his partners finding gold but neglected to say very much about those partners. I have to find them to claim my uncle's share. Now I don't have a lot of money left, but I'd be willing to pay for your time once those two men are found.'

'What exactly do you know about them and where they are?'

'Well, not much. Uncle Angus wrote about a small river with a creek flowing into it. The few names he mentioned was a place called Falling Rocks Cliff in Dark Canyon. This, he said, was east of Bear Butte.'

Starkey nodded slowly, thinking about those names. He really hadn't known anything about the Black Hills and in the short time he'd been in Fort Laramie hadn't learned much more. But he knew a couple of men who would know. Anyway, if the old man had written that much, then it was likely there was more in the letter. He'd have to be cautious, though. This woman was nobody's fool.

'Well, I'll tell you, it'd take two or three men and supplies for a week of searching to go up there. I reckon getting to Bear Butte wouldn't be a problem, but that canyon you mentioned, it's a big one. What kind of deal were you thinking about making?'

Margaret felt a load ease off her shoulders. If this man could lead her to Falling Rocks Cliff it was likely she could meet up with her uncle's partners. She'd have to be cautious, though. Going off into the wilderness with strange men could be dangerous. Her single-shot pistol might not be enough. *Oh*, she thought suddenly, *don't get ahead of yourself. What kind of deal could you make?*

'You say it'd take at least a week? Well, I should be able to afford the necessary supplies, but I don't know what to offer in the way of wages.'

'Let's figure three men and yourself. You'd have to buy a horse; we all have our own. Fact is I've an extra that I could loan you. Now, as for wages, that poses a problem. You must understand that my men, if they knew they were going to look for a couple prospectors, well, the thought of gold does funny things to some men. I'd suggest you promise a share of whatever your share is. Say ten per cent. For the three of us, that is,' he quickly added when he saw the woman frown.

Margaret leaned back in the rocker and looked out over the street. She hadn't paid much attention to it until now. Most of the buildings that she could see were built of raw, sawn planks, only a couple of them rose more than a single storey. Some, further down, were simply large tents. The street itself was cut by deep ruts left by wagons and thick with dust kicked up by the many horsemen riding here and there. As she watched, a double line of mounted blue-coated soldiers with a large-bellied sergeant riding in front came down the street. This, she shuddered to think, might become her home if she didn't find Uncle Angus's partners.

With that thought she made her decision. 'All right, ten per cent of Uncle Angus's share, or rather, my share, once we find my new partners.'

Broken Nose and the others had let Blackhand ride ahead. That suited the angry young Sioux; losing the trail of the white men was galling and he knew that even his friend, Howls at Night, was laughing at him. Let them ride slow, he grumbled to himself, he was the leader of this hunt and it was only right that he ride ahead.

What caught his eye wasn't clear for a moment, but something out of the ordinary brought him up short. Sitting his horse Blackhand let his eyes gaze around, not looking at any one thing, just taking it all in.

There . . . a streak of muddy water flowing down

the middle of that little creek. Something that wasn't natural.

He reined his buckskin beside the little river that the warriors had been following. Blackhand changed direction and pushed his buckskin into the shallow river. He climbed up the far bank and continued on, following the creek without looking behind him. He knew that sooner or later the others would follow. Meanwhile he would see what was dirtying the water. It could be the white men. Hadn't they been digging in the gravel of the river?

Con and Kincade had been digging in every spot that looked likely as they dropped down from the high country, heading for the cave camp at Falling Rocks Cliff. Not in any great hurry, they continued their search for gold. Following the creek down, with their attention more on the moving water than anything else, neither was aware of the Indian sitting his buckskin watching them.

Blackhand didn't move for a long moment; he just sat watching the two white eyes.

'Wagh,' he muttered quietly, 'they are ignorant, watching the water and not looking for danger. Come, horse, let us tell the others.'

Slowly backing up into the darkness of the forest, the Sioux leader turned back the way he had just come. When he reached the others he halted, holding up one hand.

'The white men are there,' he turned and pointed. 'They ride crazy. Quickly, half of you ride up in to those rocks. The rest will find cover on this side. When they come around that turn, we will have them.'

It felt good to be setting up his ambush, having these young unproven men do as he said. When they returned to the buffalo camp with their stories of this, he would no longer be seen as being unworthy.

The silence of the forest settled down once again until only the rustle of some small animal getting away in the brush and the constant burbling of the creek were the only sounds. For long minutes the handful of Indians, each with his bow strung and a handful of iron- or stone-tipped arrows ready, waited.

A click of iron on stone was the first sign that things were about to happen. Each warrior inhaled quietly, focusing on the two riders who came slowly into sight.

Blackhand, wanting to be the first to strike, pulled back on the yard-long cedar shaft and, aiming at the center of the shirt of the first white man, let fly.

CHAPTER TEN

Kincade was riding ahead only because Con had stopped to look at something in the fast-rushing water. As he turned to see where his young partner was, he felt the stiff feather fletching of an arrow rub his ear as the shaft buzzed past his head. Almost instinctively, the older rider threw himself from the saddle, palming his Colt and firing as he fell. Crouching behind a small pile of rocks in the middle of the creek, he yelled a warning which was lost in the yelps and loud calls coming from the rocks slightly below.

At the sound of the shot, Con was out of the saddle and grabbing his rifle, rushing forward on foot to see what Kincade had stepped into. The yelling from the attacking Indians sent ripples of fear down his back. He threw the Henry to his shoulder and fired at a flash of movement on the far side of the creek.

As arrows filled the air the two men found rocks to hide behind, rising up to take quick aim and fire when they thought it safe to do so.

Con slowed his shooting when he remembered the only shells he had were in the rifle. There was another box or two in the saddle-bags but they were on the horse and he didn't know where that animal had gotten off to.

'Hey, Con,' Kincade called out, 'how're you fixed for shells? All I got is my Colt but I got a belt-full. How are you doing?'

At his words, one of the attackers stood up, pulling back on his bow. Con shot him in the chest.

'I'm all right for a while. What happened? Are you all right?'

'Yeah, I think I turned just when that jasper shot at me. He missed.'

'Well, I've got what's in my rifle, but if they're going to be jumping up like that, I'll just wait.'

'Yeah, let them come to us. I'd reckon when their surprise didn't work they won't wait around long.'

For a long few minutes nothing moved and soon even the birds started to call to each other. Crouched down behind their rocky protection the two men waited and watched.

Then, slowly, ready to duck back, Con rose from the rocks and surveyed the hillsides.

'I think they've run,' he said, still tense and fully prepared to drop.

'Yeah, it has to be discouraging to have your ambush fail and be fighting a couple wild gunmen like us. Let's see if we can find our horses. We've still got a long ride ahead of us.'

'Yep, and I'd say we got all the gold we're going to get. From here on we'd better be paying attention.'

Blackhand watched as Broken Nose and the others rode away. The bodies of two of the younger men had been wrapped in their blankets and tied over the backs of their ponies. The young man's shoulders slumped. Missing his shot had shattered any chance that they would follow him anywhere again. Facing Spotted Tail or anyone else would not be possible. He had failed. He was no longer a warrior.

Broken Nose, riding with his shoulders square and proud led the little procession, thinking about what had gone wrong. The white men had not been ready but they still escaped the surprise attack. Blackhand was right, they should not be allowed to live. However, going up against them now would not be wise. Certainly they would be expecting another attack, but there would not be one. None of the young men riding behind him would want to face those guns again.

It would be good to have one of the firearms. He'd seen them in action before when groups of white men were hunting buffalo. The thunder and smoke left one of the shaggy beasts far off in the distance dead. Today it had been two young men, really no more than boys, dead. This sacred place, filled with the spirits of those who had gone before, was not a good place to die.

'Hey, lady, exactly what're you planning on doing with all that gold?'

Margaret didn't look at the dirty, bearded man who had gigged his horse up to ride beside her.

It was one of the two men Mr Starkey had hired, the bigger one. He had said his name was Clovis Younger and she thought that even Mr Starkey wasn't too happy about having him along. It seemed, though, that Younger knew even more about the country they were riding into than Starkey did.

The other one didn't make her feel any better. At first she thought he was just a boy, but the pearl-handled Colts looked too well taken care of for such a youngster. When she saw his eyes, she knew he wasn't a boy, they were too cold and seemed to look right through her. Starkey introduced him as Willie Nix. Both men scared her.

'Now, if'n you wanted, we could have a grand old time back at the Sutler's Saloon,' Younger said, laughing when she eventually looked at him and frowned. 'Now, lady. I ain't so bad, once I get cleaned up a mite, that is. And I know how to treat a real lady like yourself, too.'

'Hey, Clovis,' Starkey, riding along behind the woman, called softly. 'This isn't the time or the place and that woman isn't the one. Now I told you, she's leading this parade and is to be treated with respect.'

It was clear to him that he'd made a mistake in bringing these two along, but there hadn't been anyone else. He had ridden with Younger once before over in the California gold camps. The gunfighter, Nix, never seemed to get very far away from the big man. Hire one and you got the other. One benefit of bringing them along, though, was having them to blame when he came back to Fort Laramie alone. He could tell everyone it'd been the fast gunslinging kid, Nix, and old dirty Clovis Younger that'd done Angus's niece wrong. He hadn't planned on bringing anyone back with him.

For the rest of the afternoon everybody left Margaret alone with her thoughts. And she was thinking. It hadn't taken her long to realize she'd made a mistake, but it was too late to worry about it. It was done and now she'd have to deal with it.

One thing she'd done right was to purchase a

six-shot .32 Smith & Wesson revolver. The man in the post store told her he'd bought it from a man who'd used it in the Civil War.

'It don't shoot a very big bullet, ma'am,' the clerk had explained. 'that's true. But if'n you was to point this at someone it's a sure-fire thing that they'd back off. And if they didn't, wal, you've got six of these little bullets to help him change his mind.' At that the skinny-faced clerk laughed, sounding to Margaret like a horse whinnying.

After showing her how to tip the barrel back to load the cylinder and selling her a box of cartridges, she threaded the holster on to the belt of her leather riding-skirt.

None of the men knew of her single-shot derringer pistol in the pocket of her split leather riding-skirt. That, and the words of the man who had given it to her, would be her secret. Be strong and face the bullies with that strength, he'd said.

Trouble came after supper had been eaten. Younger had brought a bottle of whiskey out of a saddle-bag and was sitting across the fire, sipping it. Margaret was careful not to look at him but still was completely aware of what all three of the men were doing. Starkey and Nix were playing cards on a blanket.

Back away from the fire Margaret had used a tree branch to sweep an area clean of rocks and sticks and had laid out her bedroll. Using her saddle for a pillow, and making sure everyone could see where she had placed her revolver, she was relaxed, rereading her uncle's letter for the hundredth time. She didn't really need to read it; she'd memorized the words before ever reaching Fort Laramie. But just holding it and reading his words somehow gave her comfort.

'Now, missy, why don't you be social and have a little drink with me?' She hadn't heard Younger coming.

Steady, girl, she thought silently. He's a bully and you have to be strong.

'Clovis,' Starkey called, starting to get to his feet. 'I told you, leave her alone.'

'Ah, Stark, I ain't doing anything but trying to be friendly, offering her a drink. Ain't nothing wrong with that, now is there?' He hadn't taken his eyes off her. Holding the bottle out, he let his eyes sweep up her body but froze when he saw black hole of the derringer fixed directly on his head.

'Whoa, lady, you gotta be careful that little pistol don't go off. Now point it somewheres else.'

'No, Mr Younger, I am careful and this little pistol shoots a .44 caliber bullet, and I'm told that's big enough to blow a hole clear through you. Now back away and don't come near me again,' she said, her voice hard, cold and steady. 'Bother me any more and I will shoot you.'

Backing up with his hands out in front, one holding the whiskey bottle, Younger tried to smile but couldn't look away from the pistol. 'You wouldn't do that, now would you?' Over on his side of the fire he took another drink and then laughed. 'Yeah, maybe you would.'

Margaret leaned back, trying not to let anyone see her tremble.

Nobody said anything for a while. Younger settled down on his soogan and the poker game on the blanket continued. Margaret was just beginning to relax when she saw Starkey throw in his cards and stand up. Holding his hands away from his body, he came around the fire and, letting a smile play across his face, hunkered down on his heels.

'Well, now. You handled that pretty good. Old Angus would be proud of you. Yes sir. Now, I'll do what I can to keep them two away from you, but I doubt you'll have anymore trouble with them. That little pistol you pulled out looked mighty big.'

'Thank you, Mr Starkey,' said Margaret, sitting up and wrapping her arms around her knees. She didn't think the man could see that she still held the derringer in one hand.

'I saw you reading a letter. Would that be the one your uncle wrote?'

'Well, yes it was. Why do you ask?'

Starkey pursed his lips a bit and nodded. 'I've been thinking. I wonder if he told you anything about those two men he rode out into the mountains with?'

'No, not really, only that he had partners and they had found some gold. Placer gold, he called it.'

'Hmm,' was all that Starkey said.

'What do you know about them?' she asked.

'Oh, nothing, nothing at all. But I was just thinking, nobody knows who killed your uncle. The sheriff always said he thought it'd have to be someone who knew the old man was carrying gold and about the only ones that fit was those partners of his. Like I said, gold does funny things to some men. Now, it seems reasonable to me that someone might be looking at having half of the gold they found rather than just a third.'

He stopped and let her think on that for a minute or two. 'I wonder, would you mind if I took a look at that letter? There might be something in there that I'd see a mite different from you. I mean you being so close to your uncle and all.'

Margaret thought about what he'd said and then shook her head. 'No, there's nothing in the letter about them. I don't think Uncle Angus knew much about them either. I guess we'll have to see how they take to having a new partner before we judge what kind of men they are.'

Starkey saw he wasn't going to get the letter and got up. 'Well, I guess you're right. Better get some sleep now; we'll be riding early.'

None of the men knew the name of the river they were riding along, or even if it had a name. Riding in the lead again, Margaret let her eyes roam, taking in the beauty of the country. Tall pine trees high on the ridge to one side seemed to be swaying in a breeze. Now where they were, following a narrow game trail, the air was still.

She didn't know how long they'd been riding on that trail when she noticed how the ground was broken up. Unsure of what it could mean, she pulled up and called back to Starkey.

'Mr Starkey, should there be a lot of horse prints on this trail?'

'What? Let me see,' he said. He pushed ahead of her and swung out of the saddle. 'No, and these aren't shod horses either. That means either they're a bunch of wild stock or we've got a lot of redskins somewhere ahead of us.'

'What the hell,' snarled Younger, having come up to see what they had found. 'I don't like the idea of running into any of them red devils. This here's some holy land and they don't like it much for white folks to be riding in.'

Margaret saw that his eyes were searching the forests around them. She started to smile at his

115

nervousness when she heard a wild shriek and saw an arrow punch through the man's hat.

'Indians,' someone yelled. Starkey, still on the ground, grabbed her horse's halter and pulled it back into the trees.

'Get down and get that belt gun of yourn out. Don't go shooting unless you got a clear target, though. We don't know how many there are. Oh.' He started to turn away and then stopped. Looking back over his shoulder he smiled. 'Keep that little pistol of yours handy. Save that shot for yourself. It ain't pretty what those red devils will do to a white woman.' He drew his rifle from his saddle case, went to stand half-hidden beside a tree and watched.

'Hey, Stark,' Younger called from behind them, 'you see anything?'

'No. But they're there somewhere. You be ready.'

For a long moment nobody made a sound, and then that high yelping came again followed by shots.

'I think I got one of the buggers,' Younger called out, sounding proud of himself.

'How many you figure there are?' Willie Nix's high-pitched voice called from further back.

'Dunno. No way of telling. Just keep your head down and don't go wasting any ammunition.'

Nix's laugh was almost a whinny. 'Don't go

116

worrying about me. I don't make it a habit to miss my shots.'

Starkey was about to comment when more shots were fired. These came from further up the river.

'What the hell?' Younger cursed. 'Them redskins got guns?'

Another series of shots were fired and Starkey waited until things settled down before answering. 'No. Whoever's doing the shooting, sounds like they're on up, maybe the other side of those Indians what's attacking us.'

'Hey, anyone left alive down there?' the call cut through the quiet.

'Yeah,' Starkey yelled back. 'We're all right.'

Nothing more was said until two men came riding down the trail.

'Guess we came along at just the right time,' the older of the pair said, letting his voice carry. 'Heard your shooting and almost rode into the battle. There were half a dozen or so of the red buggers lining up ready to let go with their arrows. Con here and me opened up and caught them by surprise. Boy, did they take off.'

'Damn glad you did,' Starkey said, standing away from the tree he'd been using for cover. 'Certainly didn't expect to run into any white men up here, though.'

The two men swung out of the saddle and, keeping a short distance away, stood by their horse's heads. Margaret came to stand next to Starkey and looked them over. It was the older man who did the talking.

'Nope, neither did we. Been up here for, what, the last month or more and haven't seen anyone, except those redskins. We had a run-in with them earlier today, on further up. Leastways I expect they's the same bunch.'

Starkey nodded. 'Well, we do thank you for your help. It could've gotten bad if you hadn't come along.' He hesitated a minute, before going on, 'I'm Bart Starkey. We've been helping this young lady who's looking for a couple prospectors. Those wouldn't be you, would it? Partners of Angus Newell?'

Neither of the men said anything for a long moment and then the one called Con nodded. 'Yes, I reckon we could be. Old Angus was with us until he rode out to Fort Laramie for supplies. That was a while ago.'

Margaret gasped and stepped forward until she was facing the young stranger. 'Angus was my uncle. We've come up here in the mountains looking for you.'

'Con,' Kincade said keeping his voice low, 'I don't like the looks of this. That fella there, I've seen him before somewhere.'

'That's Mr Starkey,' Margaret said, glancing over her shoulder, 'I hired him and the others to help me find you.'

Standing there talking, they were unaware of Younger's movements until he stepped out from behind a tree and jammed a pistol in Kincade's ribs.

CHAPTER ELEVEN

'What the. . . ?'

'Now don't go moving any, buster,' Younger growled. 'Hey, boss, you know this fella? I do. I thought I'd seen him before so I snuck around to get a better look. Think back a couple years, back to the diggings on the American River over in California.'

'Hell's fire,' Starkey growled. 'I can't say as I've ever seen him before. Who're you saying he is?'

Younger chuckled but before he could answer Kincade knocked the gun barrel away, brought his fist up and knocked him down.

'All right,' Kincade yelled, pulling his Colt and earing back the hammer. 'Let's all just stand tight now. Con, it's best we get outa here. These fella's are fixing to do us some damage.'

Not understanding but sure his partner knew what he was doing, Con climbed back into the saddle and pulled his rifle. He levered a shell into the chamber and covered everyone.

'C'mon. We can talk later. Let's ride.'

Looking down the at girl, who was standing befuddled, Con nodded. He leant down and caught her around the waist. He picked her up, squeezing his thighs at the same time, sending his horse off at a gallop.

'Go, boy,' Kincade yelled. 'I'll cover you.'

The other two reined their horses around and disappeared among the trees. As soon as he could Younger drew his belt gun and fired a couple shots at the retreating men from the ground where he lay.

'Knock that off, man,' Starkey yelled. 'You'll hit the girl and we still need her. Let them go, they won't get far.'

Margaret was too surprised to do much but hold on to the arm that was keeping her from falling. The two men, getting away through the trees, slowed their rush and dropped back down on to the game trail beside the river.

'Let me go!'

'You're all right, miss,' said Con, not relaxing his hold on her twisting body. 'Don't go fighting me now or you'll hurt yourself. We'll stop up here a bit and I'll let you down.' Calling back to Kincade he laughed. 'Man, I can't recall ever seeing you move that fast before. What was that all about, anyway?'

'Let's rest our horses by that wide place and I'll tell you. I figure we were darn lucky, back there.'

At a turn in the river, the trail cut through a small patch of grass. Kincade dropped off his horse and looked back down the trail. Then he glanced at his young partner, who was lowering the young woman to the ground.

'Now what made you want to grab aholt of her? I thought you'd been taught to treat women better'n that.'

'You are both animals,' Margaret shouted, reaching in her skirt pocket for the little derringer. She pulled it and stood straight, pointing it up at her captor. 'Now get down or I'll shoot.'

Con looked first at the pistol and then at her. 'No, ma'am. I can't believe you would.' Slowly he swung down and stood facing her. 'At least not until you know more about your partners. That's what we are, aren't we, your partners?'

He turned to look over his shoulder at Kincade and nodded. 'That's the way I figure it. Something happened to Newell or this young lady wouldn't be here. I'd say something bad. I figured if we were to simply ride away from those men back there, it's likely we'd never know what. So I brought her along. But what was that all about, anyway?'

Neither man seemed to pay any attention to Margaret or the pistol she was still aiming at Con's chest, almost close enough to be touching him. For a moment she wanted to stamp her foot to remind them of her presence.

'I recognized that one what introduced himself as Starkey from over at Murphy's Camp on the American,' Kincade said, keeping watch at their back trail. 'He was using a different name then and it took me a bit to remember. He'd come into camp right after I got there. Was selling supplies from the back of a wagon and doing a good business. Sold out in one afternoon and then rode out. Wasn't gone long when a fella came walking in saying someone had stolen his wagon and goods and left him by the trail. He'd been shot and had lost a lot of blood but wasn't hurt all that bad.

'Anyway, a bunch of us went looking for the hold-up man, only to run into another man who had just been robbed. We caught up with our outlaw on down the trail a piece. Guess he didn't think we'd be after him. When he was tried by the camp's leaders and found guilty, he was sentenced to hang. Those boys didn't believe in letting a thief off easy. Well, before he could be strung up he escaped. We never did see him again.'

'No, that can't be right,' Margaret said. 'He's been working for the army as a scout. That's why I hired him to find you.' Thinking of that, she frowned. 'And now that I have found you, explain how you knew my uncle had been killed?'

'I just told you,' Con said. 'But this isn't a good time to be standing around reliving the past. Kincade, you reckon those good old boys'll be coming after us?'

Kincade thought a moment and then nodded. 'My bet is yes. Seems there's at least one reason they'll want to keep hold of little missy, here, and that's gold. Her uncle's gold. Yep, they'll be along. And don't forget, there's a passel of angry Indians somewhere out here, too.'

'Then I figure a good place to head for would be back at our camp at Falling Rock Cliffs. It's a place where we can be out of sight and which we can easily protect.' Turning to Margaret, he smiled. 'Your choice, young lady. You can ride behind old Kincade there, or with me.'

'I'll ride behind you,' she said pointing at the older man, 'but don't forget, I have my little pistol.'

Little was said as they rode on, Kincade let his horse, carrying double, take the lead and set the pace with Con dropping back to watch their rear. Spotting the little waterfall where the creek that flowed out of the upper cliffs cascaded into the river, he urged the horse across the wider water-flow and quickly found another faint trail. Eventually they reached the little grassy meadow. Margaret eased off from behind Kincade and, gently rubbing the backs of her thighs, watched the two men strip the leather off their horses.

'Well, for what it's worth, this is home,' Kincade said with a soft chuckle. 'Sorry we can't invite you to a cup of coffee, but we ran outa that treat some time ago. That was high on the list of things your uncle was going down to Fort Laramie to get.'

During the ride Margaret had decided she'd learn everything she could about her uncle and his death and felt she'd probably learn more from this man Kincade. Still angry about being grabbed, she didn't want to even look at the other one.

'I didn't know Uncle Angus,' she said, after finding a place to sit down. 'I was told by the sheriff that the three of you talked and then just rode out of town one morning.' She stopped, hoping someone would want to explain.

Kincade did. Setting on a log with his back to the cliff face so he could keep a watch over the meadow, he smiled at the girl. Con, noticing how the young woman was ignoring him, sat off to one side, leaning his back against a pine tree.

'Yep, that's about right,' Kincade said. He picked up a handful of loose dirt and he let it sift through his fingers as he talked. 'Con there and me met the old-timer there in Fort Laramie soon after we arrived. Bought him lunch, we did and it was while we was eating that he mentioned knowing a lot about this country up here. Now, we'd been talking about setting up a ranch but didn't have the money to stock one. We'd heard talk that there likely was gold up in these mountains. Ol' Angus had done some guiding a time or two and thought it was possible. So the three of us decided right then and there to come up to take a look-see.'

Careful not to take her eyes off Kincade, Margaret stretched her legs out straight in front of her and gently smoothed the thin leather skirt over her thighs. Feeling the mound made by the little pistol in a pocket made her feel safe.

'So he led you up here?'

'Yep, right here to this place. We'd had a run-in with a bunch of Indians and Con took an arrow. Wasn't much but while he healed up your uncle and I started scouting. Don't you know, after the boy was feeling better he went hunting and found the first nugget? Some people are just lucky, I guess.'

Con smiled but didn't say anything. Hearing his partner talk so much was unusual: he was always the one to set back and let the others flap their gums. Having a pretty young woman to talk to might, he thought with a silent laugh, have something to do with it. Smiling to himself he watched the light play on her hair. She was a good-looking filly, he decided. Strong-looking and firm. She'd be a hard worker, not one to sit around the parlor knitting doilies. Since she was keeping her eyes everywhere except in his direction, he was able to take his time studying her. Not beautiful, at least not what he thought of as beautiful, but confident. She'd shown that when he had grabbed her. Not a scream and not frightened. She'd do to ride the river with. But what, he wondered, made her not see how dangerous that man Starkey could be? After all, Kincade had explained about him escaping being hung. Con shook his head. He realized that the girl didn't believe his partner.

That didn't matter. Somehow this girl, really a woman, had taken a dislike of him, probably still mad about his kidnapping her. He thought it'd be best to just keep quiet and listen.

'So you did find some gold?' she asked.

'Oh, yes, that we did. Not a great amount, but that little creek Con found gave up enough for your uncle to take down for supplies. Wasn't any reason for all of us to go so while Newell rode south, we stayed up here and prospected.'

Margaret nodded. 'That's what the sheriff said: my uncle was probably killed for the gold he had. Mr Starkey thought the same.' Mentioning the man reminded her of something else. 'What about that story you told, about knowing Mr Starkey before. Was that true?'

'Sure was. Happened in a mining-camp there on the American River. He was a lot thinner then and he had a lot of face hair, but it was him all right.'

127

Margaret looked away, wondering how much to believe this man. With a beard and all, he could be mistaken. After all, from the way Starkey had been helping her, it didn't seem like he was the kind who would do what this man claimed. She thought she'd reserve judgment on that.

'The gold that my uncle took to buy supplies, was that all you found?'

'Nope. It was all we had then but not now. I'd say, now that you are taking his place in the partnership, that your third share will put you in pretty good shape.'

'Mr Starkey thinks one of you might have followed Uncle Angus into town and murdered him for the gold, so he couldn't tell anyone where the gold came from.'

Con couldn't help it; he laughed. Shaking his head he looked past the girl. 'Kincade, it's getting on toward dark. I'll go and check the horses' hobbles if you'd like to take care of some supper. I figure we've got enough of that venison left for another pot of your delicious stew.' Chuckling at his joke, he stood and walked down through the grass ignoring their guest. 'If she believes someone like Starkey, then anything you say won't matter,' he threw back of his shoulder.

Supper was a quiet affair, Margaret didn't seem to have any more questions and Kincade returned to his normal non-talkative state. Con, feeling left out but somehow able to think it was funny, simply let the silence grow.

From where they were sitting, a little apart from each other, they watched silently as the light faded and the stars came into view. The night sky was awash with little pinpricks of light. Margaret didn't remember ever seeing so many stars, she almost forgot herself and shrieked in excitement when she saw a shooting star streak across the sky. Con had been watching her in the faint light of the stars and saw her attention focus on the night sky, head tilted back and her long hair hanging softly down her back.

Working around the ranch, he hadn't met many girls his age. The only women he knew any thing about had been his mother and some of her friends who came to visit. Even in the little west Texas town where they got their supplies and the mail, there didn't seem to be any girls. Or at least any that he saw. A lot of townfolk didn't really approve of cowboys. Once he and Kincade had ridden out, they had been too busy trying to find work to spend time in hanging around any town. Con wasn't sure what he had missed out on, but watching this young woman he knew there was something.

At last, without saying anything, he spread his blankets out on a patch of ground, the same place he had swept clear of sticks and stones for himself.

Being careful not to let her catch him looking her way he spread his horse-blanket out beside the fire pit, now glowing from the embers at the bottom and, with his saddle for a pillow, lay down.

For a long time he didn't move; then, slowly, he lifted his head a little and saw that she had rolled up in her blankets and was still. Smiling, he pulled his hat brim over his eyes and went to sleep. The moon was in a late phase, with about half of it showing. It'd be coming up in a couple hours and he didn't want the extra light to bother him.

Margaret dozed a little but tried not to let herself fall asleep. Lying as she was with one of the men who might have killed her uncle across the fire from her and the other even further back at the edge of a stand of trees, she lay still, thinking.

These were the men who had been Uncle Angus's partners but she didn't trust them. After all, they had taken her away when they ran off, hadn't they? And if they were honest men, why would they tell stories about Mr Starkey? It was true she felt safer here in their camp than with that brute Younger leering at her all the time, but he'd stayed away once he'd seen she was strong. Anyway if these two really thought of her as a partner, why didn't they show her the gold mine? Coming into the camp she'd looked around and had seen the mouth of a cave. Why hadn't they slept in there? Was that where they had found the gold they said they had? Why would they want to keep that secret? After all, part of it was now hers, wasn't it?

For what seemed like hours she lay still, thinking, trying to figure out what to do. At last she made her decision. She would be strong, just like that man, Cole, had told her she'd have to be. At last, as the half-moon started showing above the tops of trees, she sat up and looked across the fire pit to where the two men were. All she could see in the shadows were black humps where she thought they had bedded down. Moving quietly, she slipped out of the blankets and pulled on her riding-boots. After settling her holstered revolver around her hips she picked up her wide-brimmed hat and slowly made her way into the darkness.

Both Con and Kincade were using their saddles for pillows but the bridles had been left hanging from a low overhanging branch. She had watched Con pull the gear from his horse and saw how he'd almost staggered when he took the full weight of the saddle and the twin bags tied to it. Margaret had ridden before, renting horses from a livery there by the school. She and her friends had spent hours riding through nearby fields and woods. Saddling a horse, however, was something she'd never done. This ride would have to be bareback.

Blackhand came awake at the sound of a horse walking near by. Crouching in the darkness of a stand of young pine trees, he watched as a rider passed on the trail below him. Only a few clouds masked what moonlight there was but from where he sat all he could make out was a shapeless figure sitting on the horse as it went by, disappearing down the trail.

A lot had happened that he did not understand and this was just another thing. It was possible, he thought, that having so many white eyes trespassing in the sacred grounds had brought out angry spirits. He shuddered to think that the unknown rider had been one of those. Not moving, he tried to think.

The day before, riding behind Broken Nose and the others, he had let his buckskin pony slow to a walk and had fallen further back. Missing the easy shot at that white man could have been the work of the spirit world. Could it be that these whites had reason to be here? Blackhand had shaken his head. That could not be. It was clear that he was not a leader of men, that was all.

Stopping to let his pony drink from the river, he had just sat with his head down feeling empty when he heard riders coming. He pulled quickly back into the cover of trees and watched as the two white men came trotting down the game trail. He strung his bow, pulled back an arrow and was about to loose it at the older man's back when he froze.

If a spirit had been protecting the younger one, would not the older one be safe? Would he miss again, his arrow not even striking the man? Uncertain and afraid of letting either of the whites know where he was, he slowly lowered the bow to rest at his side.

He and the white riders heard the far-off gunfire at the same time. The whites jabbed spurred heels into the sides of their horses and rushed out of sight. Blackhand followed slowly behind.

As he came close to where he could hear the sound of guns being fired and people yelling he reined his horse off the trail and up into the trees. After tying the single rein to a tree limb and having an arrow ready to loose, he carefully crept forward from tree to tree, stopping abruptly when one of the Indians who had followed him rushed out of the trees and continued on, fright making him blind to where Blackhand stood.

Silence filled the forest again. Faintly Blackhand heard the jabber of the whites calling out. Keeping to cover, he stole forward and found himself looking down at more white men. And a woman – one of them was a woman, standing and looking at the young man he'd seen ride by a brief time ago. This was something he didn't understand.

Suddenly, as he watched, the young man grabbed the woman and carried her away with the older man following behind. Puzzled, and keeping to the trees, the young Indian had followed.

When the three whites left the trail by the river and rode up into the upper canyon, he followed. Staying far enough away so that the horses hobbled in the grassy place didn't smell his buckskin, he sat back and continued to watch. What should he do? He could sneak closer and shoot one or another of the whites to find out if they were under the protection of a spirit. But what if they were? He could wait until dark and go steal their horses. That would be easy, but what then? Undecided, he did nothing but wait and watch.

When, some hours later, a rider went by, he thought at first it could be a spirit, but then decided it had to be one of the whites. These white-eyed people did strange things, things no one could understand. He settled back, relaxed and dozed, waiting for the sun to come up.

Riding behind Kincade, Margaret had paid attention to where they went and easily found her way back to the river. Circling around the little lake, she found the trail and gigged the horse into a trot.

'Hey, Stark, looky here. Guess who came back?' Younger called, laughing as he made a grab at the horse's bridle.

'What?' she heard Starkey yell from up in the trees. Using the ends of the reins, she slashed at

Younger's face. Howling, he let go of her horse and stepped back. Margaret kneed the horse ahead.

'Mr Starkey,' she called; then, seeing him come out of the darkness of the trees, she pulled her horse to a halt and slide down.

'Well, Miss Baldwin. We didn't expect to see you until later in the day.'

'I waited until they went to sleep and took one of their horses,' she hurried on, trying to keep pride out of her voice but failing. 'Anyway, I know where they are camped.'

'Did they show you any gold?' Younger asked, his voice thick with sarcasm.

'No, but I think I saw where they got it.'

'Now that is good news,' said Starkey. 'And you took one of their horses, did you? That means they won't be riding anywhere for a while. Good. We'll wait for full daylight and go see what we can find out.' Pointing back into the trees, he smiled. 'We set up camp back there, off the trail a piece. Your bedroll's back there and there's still a few hours till sun-up.'

'Yeah, Stark, but you said—'

'Never mind, Younger,' Starkey interrupted the man. 'Just keep an eye out. Remember, there's still a bunch of Indians out there somewhere.'

Margaret felt a little let down that her escape and the news of where she'd been taken didn't seem to matter. There were a lot of things going on that she didn't understand, but after spreading out her blankets, she realized just how tired she was, and she relaxed. A few hours' sleep and everything would probably appear clearer.

She didn't notice the man, Younger, watching her from behind a tree, a sly smile on his face as he let his eyes pass over her body. Yeah, lady, he said to himself. Get your rest 'cause you're gonna need it soon. You're mine.

CHAPTER TWELVE

'Kincade,' Con called, waking the older man up. Moonlight sent shadows across the meadow and the sun, he figured, was still a couple hours away. He didn't know what had woken him but taking a look around he'd seen that their guest wasn't in her blankets.

Coming wide awake, Con had stood for a long moment looking and listening. That was when he noticed only one horse, standing on three legs, asleep.

'C'mon, Kincade, our new partner has flown the coop and has taken your horse.'

'What? What'd you mean, taken my horse?'

'Why, you're her friend, aren't you? She would-n't ride with me. So I figure it had to be your horse she took.'

'And what,' Kincade demanded as he pulled on

his boots, 'were you doing while all this was happening?'

'Same as you, sawing logs. I reckon it was the sound of her leaving that woke me. Anyway, your horse or mine, one of them is gone. I'd say it's still a couple hours till daylight. Not much we can do until then so I'm going to take back my blankets and put them to good use.'

Kincade, standing at the edge of the trees, pursed his lips and slowly nodded. 'She's gone back to that Starkey and his gang. Only place she could go. That means they'll all be showing up come morning. The gold we told her we found will draw them like flies to a dead steer.'

'Gold *you* told her we found,' Con said, emphasizing the word.

'Yeah, I guess. But the point is we had better be ready when they come riding in. It's a long walk back to Fort Laramie with only one horse between us and carrying those saddle-bags.'

Con thought a moment and then nodded. 'All right, what do you suggest?'

'Oh, I don't see why we don't go ahead and get the rest of our beauty sleep. Doubt if anybody's gonna be showing up before sun up. Sleep light, boy.'

Con watched as his partner pulled his blanket up and then stood for a time looking out over the little grassland. Kincade was probably right but when that Starkey and his crew came calling, they'd best be ready.

There really wasn't much to be done, though, other than making sure the cartridge tubes on their two Henry rifles were full. As he took a box of .44 shells from one of the saddle-bags Con felt the few strips of venison that remained and considered whether to shovel some of it in a pocket. He decided it wouldn't matter.

The pair of leather saddle-bags with the last of the deer meat and the long shirt sleeve sack of gold were fairly light. He thought about the gold in the other bags, but he knew they were too heavy to be carrying if they had to make a run for it. Those bags had better be hidden.

'Hey, Kincade? You asleep yet?'

Grouchy and without turning to look in his direction, the older man grunted. 'Yes, of course I am. Now what?'

'I wanted you to know I was going to hide the gold in the rocks over near the cave. I'll put a little rock on top of a bigger one where the saddle-bags are. All right?'

'I guess. Now, can I get some sleep?'

'Yeah.' Grumpy old man, Con said to himself and smiled.

Hiding the heavy saddle-bags took only a minute. He'd found a small crevice that was big enough in the rocks next to the mouth of the cave and he shoved a layer of rocks over it. In the dim light all he could hope was that he'd picked a good spot.

That was about all he could think of doing. He dropped the lighter saddle-bag next to his blanket roll, then lay back with his hands behind his head. Looking up through the trees at the waning moon, he thought about the girl, Angus's niece. He was smiling as he drifted off.

There were only three warriors left to follow Broken Nose after escaping from the latest battle with the white eyes. Sitting around the remains of a small fire, with the glow of the coals making his face take on an evil cast, he thought about the trouble they were in. Returning to the band without evidence of the white eyes and without Blackhand would not be good. It was known that Spotted Tail approved of the missing leader of this little band and would not like them leaving him out in the mountains alone.

Now he was the leader and had to consider things. Riding into the buffalo camp with a white man or their scalps might make Spotted Tail forget Blackhand and smile on him, Broken Nose.

'Come,' he ordered the others, 'we must return and hunt the white men or go join the women in scraping buffalo hides.'

He stripped the hobbles off his horse and waited

until the three joined him.

'Howls at Night,' he called loud enough so all could hear, 'it is clear that Blackhand's trouble is the same as ours, the fault of the whites. We must protect this land and not leave until we do.'

Blackhand had been dozing but came instantly awake when he heard the voices of the two white men. They had discovered that the horse was missing. It came to him that the rider he had seen go by was the white woman. Wagh, he growled, if he had known that he could have caught her. A foolish white woman would be easy to catch and could show Spotted Tail and the others that he, Blackhand, could make a capture.

Closer to daylight he would try to get closer and watch these two. Killing them and taking a scalp would show the band his worth. He settled back, pulled his saddle blanket tight around his shoulders and slept.

The sound of birds calling woke Blackhand just as the first light of day was chasing the stars out of the sky. In the weak light of the moon, just before it disappeared behind the far mountain, he slowly made his way through the trees until he was close to where the two men slept. Careful not to make any noise, he settled down behind a leafy bush to see what would happen.

These were white men and they were careless in

the forest. Maybe he would be given an opportunity to redeem himself. Slowly, as the dark faded away he began to make out more detail of the white men's camp. Smiling to himself, he saw the fire pit they had dug and wondered what they had made their meals of. The sun had yet to peek over the far mountains when the two men came awake. The young Indian was amused to watch as wordlessly they sat up, put on their wide floppy-brimmed hats, pulled on boots and got out of their bedrolls. Motionless behind the bush he watched the two men roll up their blankets. When at last they spoke to one another their words were far away and muffled; all he could do was watch and wait.

Blackhand had seen white men before, but never like this. In the past he had ridden with Spotted Tail and the older braves to parley with the whites. He had been proud to be allowed to ride with the chiefs when they traveled to the log fort to make medicine with the blue-coated army chief. It was all so strange but taking his direction from Spotted Tail and the others, he had kept his eyes straight ahead. There were so many things to see and try to understand, but he knew not to let his attention waver.

Now was different. Today while he waited his chance he could watch and maybe learn. The two men didn't bother with the fire and did not stop to break their fast. Both drank deep from the creek and then, while one went out to get the horse, the other stood watching.

Attempting to figure out what they were doing, Blackhand's brow puckered with dissatisfaction when, after saddling the horse, the older man reminded the young warrior of his uncle, Black Elk. Both men were short and stocky with their head sitting square and almost against their broad shoulders as if they did not have a neck. He decided he'd call that one White Elk. The other, standing tall with his long rifle carried in the crook of his arm, was always watching down across the small pocket of grass as if waiting for something. This one he would name the Watcher.

After leaving the horse out of sight in the far trees, White Elk came back and both men hunkered down. For a long time neither man moved but each sat talking to the other, their voices just a low mumble to Blackhand's ear.

From where the Indian was he could see the black opening of a cave and to the other side, near where the horse was hidden, the rocky incline that once was a creek bed. Blackhand let his eyes roam around, taking in everything, trying to figure out what the whites had found here. This place, right up against the rough cliff, would not be a good camp for Indians. There was only one way out, and that was down the creek to the little lake. To escape if attacked someone could only run through the trees and up over the ridge or up the dry creek bed which probably led to the top of the bluff. If trouble came either way would only lead to danger; safety was too far away in either case.

Sitting cross-legged he watched and waited. The sun was three fingers above the treetops when he heard horses coming up from below. They were almost close enough for him to hear the individual animals before the two whites were aware of them. Blackhand watched as they jumped up, grabbed their long guns and ran for the rocky creek bed. By leaning forward the Indian could see those riding through the tall grass. Glancing back, he saw that White Elk and the Watcher had disappeared. He settled back to wait and see what would happen.

There were five horses coming into the camp place, carrying three men and, Blackhand saw, the woman. It was clear she had brought them to this place.

'All right, missy, where did you say they found the gold?'

This time the men had ridden right in, not getting off their horses until they were close to the fire pit. The big man who spoke was close by and Blackhand could hear every word.

The woman didn't answer but pointed. Another white man climbed off his horse and stood, taking his time to closely inspect the camp and everything around it. Blackhand thought this man was the leader and was surprised to hear him laugh.

'She means that cave, Younger. No, Miss Baldwin, that wouldn't be it. To dig a gold mine would take a lot more equipment than those two men could carry. What we're looking for is a place where they worked a creek or stream. It's placer gold they'll be finding. And that little bit of water over there is not likely.'

The woman's voice was softer and didn't carry so far. 'I thought gold came from a mine.'

The sound of the men's laughter bounced off the rocks. Blackhand couldn't understand.

'Nope, it'd be a creek like that one we followed up from the lake that we'd be looking for. We know they found gold; your uncle had a half-full poke of the stuff. All water-washed nuggets and finds. That's what the fella at the post's general store told the sheriff. Now I think those boys knew we'd be along and skedaddled. Nix, you and Younger keep a close eye out. They'll be around here somewheres. Missy here took one of their horses so they only got one. They won't be far away. Check out that cave, will ya?'

The big wide-shouldered white man shrugged and turned away toward the cliff face. Blackhand watched as the little young one, after settling his belt guns in their holsters, followed behind.

'Mr Starkey, you said before that Uncle Angus's

145

partners most likely killed him. But I've been thinking about that. Why would they? When I asked them, Mr Kincade denied it and said they had found gold and that I was to have a third of it. If what you say is true, then they wouldn't have any reason to kill my uncle. It wouldn't make sense.'

The man Blackhand thought was the leader just shook his head and laughed again. 'I think it's time to stop shilly-shallying. You've got that letter the old man sent you? There musta been something there that talks about the gold they'd found. Let me have a look at it.'

'No. I told you, there is nothing in Uncle Angus's letter about gold except to say he and his partners found a little.'

'Missy,' Starkey snarled, grabbing her wrist, 'I ain't asking, I'm telling. I've worked too hard and long on this to be put off any longer. Now give me that letter or I'll break your arm and take it.'

'Ow, you're hurting me. All right, let me go and I'll give it to you.'

'Hurry it up,' he said, releasing her and shoving at the same time.

Margaret was on the verge of crying, not so much in pain but from frustration. She had been foolish to have trusted this man. She went to her saddle-bags, dug out the letter and threw it at him.

'There. See for yourself.'

Quickly Starkey ripped the letter from the envelope and read the old man's words. 'Damn. I was sure he'd told you something.' He dropped the paper and reached out for her arm again, but missed.

'Come here, missy. Show me exactly where everything was in their camp.'

Margaret, shaking in anger, walked away from him and pointed down. 'Here's where my bedroll was and those two men were over there.'

The woman was standing close to where Blackhand crouched. Again he thought about capturing her and taking her back to the buffalo camp. He would have to wait until the white men were looking somewhere else before doing anything.

As if the leader was listening to the Indian's thoughts, he turned and walked out to the edge of the grass. Standing with his hands on his hips slowly scanned the surrounding area.

'Hey boss,' Younger yelled from the edge of the trees. 'Here's their soogans. They ain't gonna be far away.'

'Wal, keep your eyes open,' the leader called from where he stood. 'I figure these jaspers to be tricky.'

For a long moment there was no sound. The leader stepped further out to stand looking up at the cliff and the woman remained standing next to the fire pit. Blackhand saw she had a deep frown furrowing her forehead. The other two men had gone out of sight in the cave. Now was a good time to seize her.

CHAPTER THIRTEEN

The moment Blackhand stood to make his rush toward the white woman he was thinking of nothing else and wasn't aware of things erupting around him. Keeping his eyes on her, he didn't see the big man coming out from the cave, a pair of leather saddle-bags thrown over one shoulder. That man didn't hesitate but quickly ran toward his horse. Starkey was just turning back toward the camp when he saw the young Indian come busting out of the bushes.

'Hey,' he called and started to run, only to stop when he heard someone call from behind him. Twisting around, he saw old man Angus's partners coming from behind a pile of rocks. One, the younger one, came striding toward him. The other one had turned to run into the trees.

'Starkey,' Con called as he walked. 'I think it's about time you told Miss Baldwin there what

149

happened to her uncle.'

Starkey laughed. 'Hey, this is turning out to be a good day all around. Here you are, coming out to welcome us into your camp. Now, you tell me, where's the gold. The old man gave up what he had and it's for damn sure that girl ain't going anywhere with what you've found. So what say you stop right there and let me show you how I deal with the likes of you.'

But Con didn't stop. He didn't even slow down. Walking steadily closer he saw Starkey suddenly realize that he was getting too close. Panicked, the big man pulled at his holstered revolver. That was when Con lifted the barrel of the rifle he was carrying at his side and thumbed the hammer. The bullet caught Starkey in the chest, knocking him back. Con, still coming on, levered another round into the chamber and without aiming touched the trigger, driving Starkey back another step before knocking him flat on his back.

Then he saw Margaret, standing looking down at a body. As if coming out of a fog, he heard horses running and looked toward the trees in time to see one of Starkey's men lying low across the neck of his racing horse with Kincade right behind him.

Con took off running toward the woman, not bothering to look at Starkey as he hurried past.

'I . . . I shot him,' she said hesitantly as he halted

150

next to her. 'He was coming at me with that knife and I . . . I shot him.' She turned away and fell into Con's arms.

Looking over her shoulder he saw the young Indian lying with his arms outstretched, a long-bladed wooden-handled butcher knife grasped in his hand. A bewildered look was frozen on his face.

'You're all right. You did what you had to do.'

'A man named Cole gave me this pistol,' she said, stepping away and holding her little derringer out, 'and told me to be strong if anyone tried to do me harm. Wait until he got close and then shoot, he said. I've been carrying it since I boarded the train. I didn't think I'd have to use it or even wonder whether I could. Oh,' she glanced at the body, 'I didn't even think. I just did what Cole said.'

Con let a sad smile lift his lips. 'That's what happens out here in the wild country. We all do just what we have to.'

Glancing around, he pursed his lips. 'Now I've got to go see what kind of trouble my partner is getting himself into. You stay here and—'

'No,' she interrupted him, 'I can't stay here with . . . with that.'

'I won't argue with you. Come on.' Con ran to where Starkey's horse was ground-hitched and jumped into the saddle. 'Get your horse and follow me,' he called, jabbing heels in the horse's side.

Con kept low over the horse's neck as he pushed the animal as fast as he could through the trees, racing down the game trail. Looking ahead he could see where those horses running ahead of him had churned up the ground. He expected to run into Kincade or his horse at any turn but didn't catch sight of him until getting near where the creek fell into the pond. Then, as he came around a huge pine tree he saw his partner standing next to his horse, using his saddle to rest his rifle on, aiming it further downstream.

'It's that kid what was riding with Starkey. I think the other one's further down,' he hollered as Con pulled up and jumped out of the saddle. 'Look at him, just standing there, like he was a big man.'

Con looked through the brush at where Kincade was pointing. Nix stood with his legs spread, knee-deep in the creek, his back straight, his hands hovering close to the pearl handles of his six-guns.

'C'mon, you heathens,' he was yelling. 'Let's see just how brave you really are. Go ahead, make your play and you'll find out just what a gunslinger can do. Go on, dammit. Make your play.'

'What the hell's he doing?' Con asked bewilderedly.

'I think he's run into a few of those Indians what've been causing so much trouble. Looky there, beyond his shoulder. There are three or

152

four of them facing him with their bows and arrows. Lordy, if'n I was him I'd be ducking for tall timber. Them boys can be mean.'

CHAPTER FOURTEEN

Con heard a horse coming behind him and stepped back. It was Margaret. He grabbed her reins and motioned her to keep quiet. He was just turning back to see what was happening when he heard one of the redskins let out a yell.

Nix made his draw, pulling both revolvers up, firing as fast as he could. The sound was like a roll of thunder. Most of the bullets tore up the stream in front of him as arrows struck him in the chest, turning his body until he faced upstream. Somehow the gunman's fingers continued to pull the triggers, Con could hear the hammers hitting empty shells until he fell face down in the water.

The forest was silent until Kincade cursed. 'Damn, those Injuns are gone. I'll bet they've gone on after that other one. Come on, Con. He's got the saddle-bags with the gold.'

KIncaid threw himself into the saddle and hammered his heels against the horse's side. Con glanced back at Margaret, stuck a boot into the stirrup and barely found the saddle before his horse took off.

Angling into the forest at the edge of the creek, the two cowboys had nearly overrun the Indians, who were on foot. Before his horse stopped, skidding on its hocks as the rider jumped off, Kincade was kneeling with his Henry aimed at the nearest warrior. In a flash Con was beside him, swinging his rifle up. His horse, breathing heavily, wandered off a ways, head hanging.

'What. . . ?' he started to ask but stopped when Kincade fired, dropping one of the warriors. Somewhere ahead another Indian started yelling. Catching movement through the trees, Con saw Younger trying to escape by jumping from rock to rock across the creek at the head of the waterfall.

Kincade fired at another of the Indians and cursed when he missed. Con, trying to find a target, held his fire. Both men watched as the big man slipped on a wet rock and fell into the creek. Seeing their victim struggling to get to his feet, Broken Nose and those who were left of his men rushed forward, firing arrow after arrow.

Con and Kincade joined in, firing as fast as they could lever shells and pull triggers. Younger eventually struggled to his feet and turned to face the red men, rifle in one hand and the leather saddle-bags still hanging heavily over a shoulder. Snarling, he was trying to bring his weapon up when an arrow struck him in the chest. Both the white man and the last standing Indian fell into the fast-rushing water, their bodies rolling a little as they were washed over the falls and into the pond.

After all the shouting and shooting, the silence seemed to Con to be intense. Slowly, as he stood up and turned to look at Margaret sitting her horse, his hearing cleared. The only sound was the gurgling of the creek.

'Looks like that's the last of your hired guides,' he said, shaking his head.

'I heard what Mr Starkey said about Uncle Angus, back there before . . . before you shot him. I shouldn't have believed him when he said you and Mr Kincade were the murderers.'

'Mr Kincade.' The younger man snorted. 'Now that's a first. Con, maybe it's about time I changed my name,' he chuckled as he walked over to his horse. Rubbing the animal's nose, he said it again. '*Mister* Kincade. Horse, let's have a little respect from you from now on. I'll Mister Kincade you, old man. But don't you think we ought to be looking to see if that fella didn't drop those saddle-bags there in the creek?'

'By the Almighty, I clean forgot them in all the

excitement.' Kincade gave the horse a final pat and turned back to the creek. He pulled off his boots, gingerly waded out and started searching the water where Younger had slipped and fallen.

'They ain't nothing here, Con.'

'Those saddle-bags'll be heavy. They have to be there somewhere.' Sitting on a rock, Con drug his boots off and waded out in the knee-deep water. Back and forth the two men rummaged around the rocky creek bottom, finding nothing.

At last both men, standing at the very edge of the falls, stood and looked down into the deeper water.

'That's where they went, sure as shooting.'

'*Mister* Kincade,' Con asked softly, 'do you want to go in there, see if you can find them?'

'Nope, never did learn to swim. Now a young man such as yourself should be able to jump in easily enough.'

'Ha. This is as deep as I want to get in any water. You know, I'll bet there's a lot of gold down there, at the bottom. Gold that's been washed down over the years.'

'Far as I'm concerned, it can stay there. C'mon, I'm getting wet.'

Back at Falling Rock Cliff, Con and Kincade dragged the bodies of Starkey and Blackhand back into the trees out of sight.

157

'Aren't you going to bury them?' asked Margaret, then said nothing more when the two men didn't bother answering.

'Hey, looky here,' Kincade called after inspecting the saddle-bags behind the horse that Starkey had been riding. 'Con, we got us some coffee.'

'We had a lot of supplies.' Margaret spoke up. 'That's about the last of it, though.'

'Well, there's a little of that venison left and with this bit of coffee, we can eat like kings.' Glancing at the woman, he smiled, 'And a queen.'

Later, in the early afternoon, the three with a string of horses following behind started south toward Fort Laramie. Kincade watched as Margaret rode alongside his young partner. They looked good, he decided, riding along together and talking.

Margaret fell silent for a while, then looked over at Con. 'I want to apologize for not trusting you before.'

'No reason to. How were you to know that Kincade back there and me were good people. Your uncle fit in pretty good with us and would have made a good partner. He liked the idea of being part of the ranch we've been thinking about.'

'What will you do now?'

'Well, I think we've had enough of looking for gold. Had enough of these mountains too, for that

158

matter. Fact is, we're not coming out of here exactly broke.' He looked over at her and smiled. 'Before we found that pocket of gold that filled the saddle-bags, we'd found enough to put in a little sack I made from a shirtsleeve. You get your uncle's share and that will get you back East and enough to live on for a while, until you can get settled.'

Neither said anything for a while.

'I don't think I'll return to the city,' Margaret said at last. 'There's nothing there for me.' She sat loosely in the saddle for a bit then glanced over at Con again. 'What about that ranch you and Kincade were hoping to put together? Are you still going to do that?'

'I don't know if we can. We'll have the fellow at the post's general store weigh out what gold we've got and then see. A third of it is yours.'

'Do you think there'll be enough left to buy your ranch?'

'Oh, I suppose we could put something together. A bit south, down in the Indian Territory, there's some land to be had and all we'd need is to stock it.'

Margaret nodded. Be strong, she told herself. If you want something, be strong and ask for it. 'Well, you say we're partners,' she started and then, not letting herself stop, went on. 'What would happen if we stayed partners and used all the gold to do that? Go south and start a ranch.'

Con looked at her while he thought about what she'd said.

'Margaret, I . . . well, I guess it's something to think about.'

Meeting his eyes, she smiled. 'Back East my friends, my good friends, called me Maggie.'

Not looking away, he nodded. 'I think I want to be more than just good friends. I'll call you Margaret.'

Kincade had heard part of the conversation before he slowed his horse, dropping back to give the couple some room. Watching them looking at each other he smiled. Things were likely to work out right nice, he chuckled. Yes sir, right nice.